TURPITUDE

Detectives investigate a sinister murder in this gripping Scottish mystery

PETE BRASSETT

Paperback published by The Book Folks

London, 2019

ISBN 978-1-6969-5099-2

www.thebookfolks.com

TURPITUDE is the tenth novel by Pete Brassett to feature detectives Munro and West. Details about the other books can be found at the end of this one. All of these books can be enjoyed on their own, or as a series.

Prologue

Since relinquishing her role as a support teacher at the Kyle Academy – a stressful occupation which involved nurturing the needs of failing pupils – Peggy McClure, a fifty-two-year-old gym bunny with more muscle than a presidential cavalcade, had, without the need for surgery, replaced her tired, lacklustre expression with the happy-go-lucky grin of somebody enjoying an illicit affair with a five litre tub of whisky ice cream.

Freed from the anxiety of worrying about her charges' progress, she embraced each day as an employee of the council's waste division with the verve of a drunk in a dive bar, safe in the knowledge that, barring a fire, flood, or fatality, whatever happened at work would never be enough to keep her awake at night.

Unlike the quarry-deep landfill site at Tarbolton, a sprawling excavation marring an otherwise unsullied landscape, the recycling centre at Heathfield was an enclosed warehouse-style complex where members of the public were free to dispose of anything from cardboard, glass, and aluminium, to fridges, furniture, and garden waste. However, for the tardy few who arrived after hours, the easiest option – despite warning signs to the contrary –

was to dump the rubbish by the gates, an action invariably rewarded with a letter from the council accompanied by a still from the security cameras and a fine of two hundred pounds for illegal fly-tipping.

Not one to procrastinate, Peggy heaved the usual assortment of miscellaneous junk – a filthy mattress, a stainless steel sink, a car battery, two propane gas cylinders, one dilapidated wardrobe and a pile of bulging bin bags – into the compound while her colleague, the substantially younger and altogether not unattractive Gordon Miller, busied himself with a pair of gloves.

Delivering a playful pat on the back, she joined him on a reclaimed garden bench and began the arduously unpleasant task of sifting through the plastic sacks in search of something that might identify the owner.

Swathed in a scuffed hi-vis jacket, Miller, who'd harboured a secret desire for the enigmatic bottle-blonde ever since she'd joined the team, cast her a sideways glance and smiled as he ripped open one of the bags.

Of all the employees, Peggy McClure was the only one not to whinge, whine, or moan about the work. Of all the women on the site, she was the only one who could fire a barrage of cheeky one-liners at a good-looking fellow if asked where he should dump his antiquated collection of VHS tapes. And of all the people he'd ever known, Peggy McClure was the only one whose glass was always half full unless, of course, it was a Friday night at the Redstone Inn, when the opposite was true.

Reeling at the pungent aroma of what she assumed to be the fetid corpse of a chicken well past its use-by date, she carefully picked her way through the array of stinking food trays, beer bottles, and soiled nappies before retrieving a large tin of dog food and waving it under Miller's nose.

'Here,' she said with a wink and a grin. 'That's not something you'll find listed under ingredients.'

Chapter 1

As one of the umpteen unfortunates left wallowing in a mire of self-pity after the unforeseen demise of a loving relationship, DI West, whose emotional state was all the more precarious thanks to the misogynistic attitude of her male colleagues whilst previously policing the streets of London, attempted to hasten her return to independence by rejecting the advances of would-be suitors and choosing instead to share her bed with a bottle of vodka, before spending a torturous week surviving on a vegetarian diet in the Buddhist environs of the Holy Isle in a last ditch attempt to regain her sanity.

However, of all the therapies available, self-prescribed or otherwise, it was the metaphorical if not unexpected kick up the backside from her mentor's size twelve boot that not only encouraged her to focus on her career but to follow him back to Scotland where, he'd assured her, the only glass ceiling she was ever likely to encounter was that of Edinburgh's Waverley station.

Content that the now retired but indefatigable James Munro was well enough to fend for himself since undergoing major heart surgery, she sat clad in a white tee shirt, black jeans, and waxed cotton biker jacket, tucking into a bacon butty whilst DS Dougal McCrae, fresh from a weekend's fishing on the banks of Kilbirnie Loch, talked her through the moped-mounted antics of an apparently hapless duo of would-be thieves who, for the third time in as many weeks, had fled empty handed when confronted by the owners of a petrol station, the kebab shop on the High Street, and a convenience store.

'All we do know,' he said, 'is that the moped was stolen.'

'There's a surprise,' said West. 'Do we know who from?'

'Aye, they nicked it off a fella delivering pizza to a house on Bellevue Crescent about a month ago, but see here, miss, there's one thing I don't get. They're not armed.'

'Dream on. I don't think there's much call for pacifists in the criminal world.'

'Aye, that's my point,' said Dougal. 'I mean, look at all those neds down in London, they're waving machetes around like a bunch of demented peasants, but not these numpties. I'm beginning to think they've been carrying out a few dry runs before attempting something bigger.'

'You might be right,' said West. 'Better keep an eye on Mothercare. Have we got any idea who they are?'

'We have,' said Dougal with an incredulous grin. 'Get this: before they tried robbing the petrol station, they tanked up the moped and paid for the fuel with a debit card. I'm just waiting on the bank for some details.'

'Dear, dear, dear,' said DC Duncan Reid, yawning as he raised his head from the desk. 'They're obviously not the sharpest tools in the shed. Get a list of all the traffic wardens in the area, you'll find them there.'

West, recognising the sound of laboured footsteps in the corridor, sat bolt upright as the door flew open.

'Bent traffic wardens?' said DCI Elliot. 'Is there any other kind?'

With his towering frame and enormous bulk, George Elliot, known affectionately as 'The Bear', had a reputation for instilling the fear of God into those who crossed his path but was, in reality, a deskbound DCI who put the welfare of his team, and his appetite, before all else.

'I smell bacon,' he said. 'I don't suppose…'

'Sorry sir,' said West, 'that little piggy's gone to market.'

'Pity. Mrs Elliot's been plying me with a half a grapefruit and a wee bowl of granola of a morning and I'm telling you, it's not enough. What's wrong with porridge, for goodness sake?'

'Nothing at all. I like mine with a huge dollop of jam.'

'Jam?' said Elliot. 'Careful, Charlie. You're messing with something of national importance here. I'd keep that to yourself if I were you. Now, I'm here for a reason.'

'Go on.'

'If it's not inconvenient, I need to borrow Detective Constable Reid. It won't take long.'

'No bother,' said Duncan. 'What's the story?'

'Follow me and you'll find out.'

'Uh-oh,' said Dougal with a smirk. 'I hope you've been practising the Fosbury flop because it looks like you're for the high jump.'

* * *

When he was a recalcitrant youth, raging against the establishment, there was little doubt in his teachers' minds that Duncan's only hope of employment would be as a labourer on a building site or as a docker at the Ocean Terminal in Greenock.

Angered that his potential should be measured purely by his ability to put pen to paper, and the stark realisation that not all police officers had to wear a uniform, he enrolled at Tulliallan college and, much to their surprise, graduated two years later by the skin of his teeth.

However, despite his newfound role as poacher turned gamekeeper, he refused, albeit unintentionally, to address senior figures with the deference their rank demanded, treating them instead in much the same way he would a pal in a pub, an action which invariably resulted in the forging of a mutually respectful relationship.

'I'm with you on the porridge thing,' he said, slumping in his seat, 'but I'd lay off the granola if I were you.'

'Is that so?'

'Oh aye. It's loaded with sugar. I'd give it up before your teeth start falling out.'

'I never realised,' said Elliot, unable to contain his glee. 'So, it's not that healthy after all?'

'It is not. It's high in calories too. No disrespect, but that's the last thing you're needing.'

'That's what I've been telling her!'

'You should get your missus to read the packet, that'll put her right.'

'I will,' said Elliot. 'I will indeed. Now, down to business.'

'Oh aye. What is it? Are you needing some furniture moved or something?'

'No, no. It's about your exam.'

Duncan glanced at Elliot with a casual shake of the head and slowly raised his hand.

'You're alright,' he said. 'I knew I shouldn't have taken it. I'm not that good at revising or writing things down. I never have been.'

'Well, some folk are more adept at taking a practical approach to policing.'

'Aye, that's me,' said Duncan. 'Practical. I'm not fussed, I'm happy as I am. I might give it another shot next year.'

'No need.'

'How so?'

'You've passed,' said Elliot. 'Eighty-seven per cent. That's high enough for them to mark your grade as exceptional.'

'Are you joking me?'

'I kid you not.'

'Well, I didn't see that coming. Are you sure you're not confusing me with somebody else?'

'Positive,' said Elliot, 'but here's the thing. I hate to rain on your parade, laddie, but I'm now faced with something of a dilemma.'

'And what's that?'

'What do I do with another DS?'

Duncan took a deep breath and scratched the back of his head.

'I see your point,' he said. 'You can't have two of us rattling about the place. So how does this work?'

'Unfortunately,' said Elliot, 'it's not up to me. The powers that be will post you where you're needed.'

'So, I could end up anywhere?'

'Indeed.'

'I'm not sure I like the sound of that,' said Duncan. 'Look, let's just forget about this whole sergeant thing, okay? Like I say, I'm happy where I am.'

'You are giving up too easily,' said Elliot, 'and from what I hear, that's not like you at all.'

'So, what's the plan?'

Elliot leaned back, clasped his hands around his ample belly, and stared pensively at the ceiling.

'I shall say we're understaffed,' he said, 'and that you are an indispensable member of the team that we simply cannot afford to lose.'

'Will that work?'

'Perhaps. I could tell them we were four, that we've already lost Munro, and that if they transfer you we'll be down to two, but that's where things might backfire.'

'How so?'

'With just Charlie and Dougal in the office there's a good chance they'll transfer operations somewhere else.'

'Oh no,' said Duncan, waving a finger as he made for the door. 'I'm not being responsible for that. No, no. Let's leave things as they are.'

'I'm sorry,' said Elliot, 'but as I say, it's not up to me. Look, this was supposed to be a happy occasion, so I apologise for taking the edge off it. Leave it with me, I'll do my best.'

'If you say so.'

'And tell Charlie I need a word.'

* * *

'Oh good, you're back,' said Dougal. 'Jeez-oh, going by the look on your face you must've got quite a rollicking.'

'Quite the opposite,' said Duncan as he reached for the kettle.

'How so?'

'You'll find out soon enough. Anyone for a brew?'

'Yeah, go on,' said West. 'I'm parched.'

'Oh, I nearly forgot, miss. The Bear, he wants to see you.'

'Now?'

'Aye.'

'In that case, do me a favour. There's some crazy woman downstairs desperate for a word about something or other. Sort her out, would you?'

Chapter 2

Rankled by Elliot's pessimistic forecast and doubtful of his senior's ability to convince the bureaucrats at divisional headquarters that a second DS would be better than none, Duncan – castigating himself for jeopardising the future of the unit – made his way downstairs and slipped silently into the foyer, his mood buoyed by the sight of a slender blonde wearing cargo pants and a tight white vest pacing the floor and looking, contrary to West's description, anything but deranged.

'Hello there,' he said as he leant against the door.

Peggy stopped in her tracks, slowly turned around, and warily eyed the stubble-ridden scruff standing before her.

'Sorry, son,' she said, 'I'm not being funny, but shouldn't you be in your cell?'

'I should,' said Duncan, 'but they let me out so's I could stretch my legs.'

'Well, if you don't mind, I'm waiting for someone.'

'Oh aye? Are you on a promise?'

'Not that it's any of your business,' said Peggy, 'but I'm waiting for a detective. The fella on the desk said someone was on their way.'

'Well, I'm here,' said Duncan. 'DS Reid, at your service.'

'You? But you don't look like a detective.'

'How so?'

'Should you not be wearing a tie? And have a big beer belly? And no hair?'

'You watch too much telly, Miss…'

'McClure. Peggy McClure.'

'Right then, Miss McClure. What's the story?'

Peggy held out her hand and proffered a blue plastic carrier bag, knotted by the handles.

'This,' she said. 'I'd hold your breath if I were you, it's honking.'

Unfazed by the odour, Duncan unfurled the knot, reached inside, and retrieved a tin bearing the face of a large black Labrador.

'Don't tell me,' he said, 'your doggy opened this himself and scoffed the lot while your back was turned.'

'Not quite,' said Peggy, 'there's something in there not even he would touch.'

Duncan glanced at Peggy, pulled back the ring-pull, and peered inside.

'Well,' he said with a smirk, 'I've heard of biting the hand that feeds you, but this is taking things a bit too far, don't you think? Where did you find this?'

'At work.'

'Which is?'

'The recycling centre, over at Heathfield.'

'And there was I thinking it was only the NHS that recycled body parts. We need to have a wee chat, are you okay for half an hour?'

'Aye. No bother.'

* * *

'Well, well, well,' said West as Duncan sauntered into the office. 'If it isn't our very own dark horse.'

'Sorry?'

'I've just been having a chat with Elliot.'

'I see,' said Duncan. 'So, he's told you the bad news?'

'Bad news?' said Dougal. 'Jeez-oh, have you lost the plot, *Sergeant*? It's cracking news!'

'It is not.'

'How so?'

'Did he not tell you I might get shipped off somewhere else?'

'Sure did,' said West.

'And did he not tell you we might get shut down?'

'Yup. And did he not tell you, you worry too much?'

'Sorry, miss,' said Duncan, 'but this is no laughing matter, this is serious. What if…'

'Life's too short for what-ifs,' said West. 'Have some faith, he'll sort it, don't you worry. I wouldn't be surprised if he gets Jimbo on-board to fight your corner too. Now, stop moping about, what's up with the fruit-loop downstairs?'

'And what's in the bag?' said Dougal, 'I hope it's biscuits because I'm feeling peckish.'

'Then you're in luck,' said Duncan, 'here you go. Chocolate fingers, only without the chocolate.'

Preparing himself for what would undoubtedly be a practical joke, Dougal looked quizzically at the tin before peeking inside and retching at the contents.

'Actually, I'm not that hungry just now. I think I'll wait.'

Fearing his breakfast may not make its way along the digestive tract the way nature intended, Dougal remained behind his desk while West and Duncan sat silently regarding the dismembered digits like a couple of budding naturalists waiting for an egg to hatch, until West, taking up the gauntlet, shattered the silence by snapping on a latex glove and prodding one of the fingers like a dead goldfish.

'So,' she said, 'whoever these belonged to obviously had a good holiday, that's a heck of a tan he's got.'

'He?' said Dougal from behind his screen. 'What makes you think it's a fella?'

'Of course it's a fella! Look at the bleeding size of them! Although, I have to say, he could've done with a manicure.'

'Those two,' said Duncan, jabbing them with the tip of his biro, 'look like an index finger, and a middle finger. And I'm guessing whoever owned these was right-handed.'

'What makes you think that?'

'The index finger has nicotine stains halfway down the right-hand side, which match those on the left of the middle finger.'

'Oh, that's good,' said West. 'That's very good, indeed. So now we know he's a smoker, too.'

'Aye, roll-ups, probably.'

West arranged the fingers in a neat row, aligning them by the severed edge.

'There's something else,' she said. 'These were all chopped off at the same time, and whatever did it was bloody sharp. That's a hell of a clean cut.'

'Aye, you're not wrong there,' said Duncan. 'Probably a cleaver, or one of those big butcher's knives. The thing is, where's the fourth one? The pinkie? Surely he'd have lost that too?'

'Maybe the dog had it, after all. Right, Dougal, bag these up and get them over to our friendly pathologist. Maybe McLeod can tell us when they were cut off and how old they are. Duncan, what's the situation with the woman who found them?'

'That's a Miss Peggy McClure,' said Duncan, 'she works at the recycling plant. These were dumped outside the gates with a heap of other stuff. She's already called the centre and they've shut-up shop until we're done. I'm heading over there now to get a copy of the CCTV, then I have to sift through all the other crap.'

'Blimey, there's no stopping you now, is there?'

'I may as well make the most of what time I have left. Dougal, do you fancy getting your hands dirty, pal?'

Dougal thought for a moment, then curled his lip and shook his head.

'No, you're alright,' he said. 'It's probably best if I stay here...'

'Why am I not surprised?'

'...so I can start looking for Captain Hook. He must have been treated somewhere, the hospital maybe, or one of the GP surgeries.'

'How about you, miss?'

'You bet!' said West. 'I'm always up for a game of poker.'

'Poker?'

'Yeah, two more of these and we'll have a full hand.'

'Dear God. I'll drive.'

Chapter 3

As an inquisitive individual who'd spent every waking hour, much to the annoyance of his late wife, deliberating the whys and wherefores of unsolved cases, Munro, in retirement, found the lack of anything cerebrally challenging to occupy his time as frustrating as trying to scrape the last dregs from the bottom of a jar of Marmite.

Having applied a final coat of gloss to the woodwork in his recently refurbished kitchen – a room which, though pleasant enough, lacked the scuffed, stained, and splintered charm of the original – he ventured outside where any plans he'd harboured of alleviating the boredom by weeding, pruning, and watering the garden were swiftly scuppered by a not unwelcome call from an anxious DCI Elliot.

'George,' he said. 'To what do I owe the pleasure?'

'Pleasure?' said Elliot with a huff. 'My life's devoid of pleasure just now, James, but that's another story. How the devil are you?'

Munro, blinded by the sun glinting off the sea, placed his trowel on the dry stone wall, and paused before speaking.

'If I'm honest,' he said, 'I'm not great. I'm not great at all.'

'Good heavens man, what does that mean? Is it your heart? Dear God, will I call for an ambulance?'

'No, no,' said Munro, 'it's nothing a decent crossword or a John Doe couldnae fix.'

'Thank goodness for that, you had me worried,' said Elliot. 'It sounds to me like you could use some company. A wee spot of lunch, perhaps? Are you up to driving?'

'I am. What's the catch?'

'Catch? Why does there always have to be a catch?'

'Because I know you better than you know yourself, George. You're more transparent than a plate glass window.'

'Nonetheless, lunch it is. Will twelve o'clock do you?'

'If you're buying,' said Munro, 'I can be there by eleven.'

* * *

Apart from a hulking George Elliot wedged behind a table who, without his tie or epaulettes, had the presence of a gangland boss awaiting an audience, the restaurant – a traditional Italian opposite the leafy Wellington Square – was completely empty.

Munro took a seat, poured himself a glass of sparkling mineral water and, ignoring the menu, ordered lunch with strict instructions that any accompanying vegetables be replaced with an extra serving of French fries before his plate reached the table.

'Are you sure you should be eating that?' said Elliot, waving his knife. 'I mean, after the operation and all?'

'Och, away!' said Munro. 'Do you think I'm going to sit here nibbling on lettuce leaves while you tuck into a Bistecca alla Fiorentina? No, no. A well-done sirloin's not going to kill me, and if it does, I cannae think of a finer way to go. So, what's the problem?'

Deeming his dry-aged Aberdeen Angus a fee rather than a blatant bribe for ghost-writing a glowing appraisal of DS Duncan Reid's exceptional ability and as yet unfulfilled potential as a detective, Munro – judging his services to have been grossly under-valued – ordered a bowl of apple pie and vanilla ice cream as the waiter cleared the table.

'Count your blessings we didnae meet this evening,' he said.

'How so?'

'Because it would have cost you a Barolo and a couple of twelve-year-olds as well.'

'There's always next time,' said Elliot, raising his glass. 'So, you'll send me an email, then? With your thoughts?'

'Email?' said Munro. 'Are you joking me? No, no, you'll receive a hand-written draft just as soon as I have one ready. You can ask one of your minions to type it up.'

'That'll be Mrs Elliot, then. Dear God, I'd best fetch her something on the way home or she'll accuse me of exploitation.'

'Incidentally,' said Munro as he shovelled a spoonful of ice cream into his mouth, 'I've not heard from Charlie, she must be busy.'

'Aye, she and the rest of them,' said Elliot. 'Duncan's taken her off to the recycling centre, they're looking for body parts.'

Munro, sensing the elusive John Doe had arrived in town, polished off his pie and listened intently.

'Some lassie found three fingers amongst the rubbish earlier this morning, so they've gone to look for the other two. Or a hand. Or an arm. Who knows?'

'If we were in Saudi Arabia,' said Munro, 'I'd not bat an eyelid, but this has all the hallmarks of a revenge attack. Not unlike the Yakuza.'

'If you say so, James.'

'Is that it?'

'I wish it were,' said Elliot, 'but we've also had a couple of neds on scooters trying to hold up a shop or two; all without success, I might add, until…'

'Until?'

'Until I left the office. The jewellers on Newmarket Street.'

'A good, old-fashioned smash and grab?'

'Aye, it looks that way, but I've a terrible feeling it's about to turn into a murder inquiry.'

'How so?'

'The owner,' said Elliot. 'He's in the hospital.'

'So, he's injured?'

'That's an understatement. He took a blow to the head. With a lump hammer. I'm not sure how much of it he has left.'

'Well, you've certainly got your hands full,' said Munro, 'I'll give you that. Carry on like this and they'll not refuse Duncan a permanent posting, that's for sure.'

'I hope you're right,' said Elliot, 'we need him now more than ever. In fact, we could use all the help we can get.'

'Here it comes.'

'I don't suppose…'

'You get the bill, and I'll walk you back.'

* * *

With a large Americano and a chocolate fudge brownie intensifying an uncontrollable surge of adrenalin, Dougal – as tense as a terrier in a neutering clinic – hovered behind his desk, frantically trying to locate the address of a moped mugger on one computer whilst attempting to trace a vehicle spotted at the scene of the armed robbery on the other.

'Boss!' he said as Munro ambled through the door. 'Am I glad to see you! How are you keeping?'

'Well, I've a pulse and a full belly, so I cannae complain.'

'I could,' said Dougal. 'My head's mince.'

'So, you're busy then?'

'Busy? I'm pure frazzled!'

Munro, seizing the opportunity to wheedle his way into the investigation, hung his coat over the back of a chair and sat down.

'So,' he said. 'What's the story?'

'Jeez-oh,' said Dougal. 'Where shall I begin? How about the raid on the jewellers?'

'Was that not a couple of chaps on scooters?'

'I wish it were. After three failed missions I was convinced it was, but no. It's not them.'

'You're sure?'

'Aye, boss. I'm positive. You see, the fellas riding the mopeds always operate as a pair, but this fella was on his own. Plus, he had a motor, not scooter. And, he made no attempt to hide his face, in fact, he was pure brazen.'

Munro stood, loosened his tie, and walked towards the window with his hands clasped firmly behind his back.

'What have you got so far?'

'Well,' said Dougal, sighing as he fell to his seat, 'the robber's about five feet, ten inches tall, slim build, and he was wearing blue jeans and a checked shirt. He's got brown hair, medium length, and he took off in a small, white hatchback with a black cross on the front.'

'A cross? Like the Saltire? Or a crucifix?'

'I've no idea, boss.'

'Then you need to speak to the witness and get more detail.'

'I would if I knew who he was,' said Dougal. 'He didn't give any contact details; said he didn't want to get involved.'

'So much for community spirit.'

'Apart from that, we've only got the first part of the index: Sierra Golf, one-eight. I'm doing my best to trace it now but it's not going to be easy.'

'And how about the raid?' said Munro. 'Does it look as though it was calculated or impulsive?'

'Hard to say,' said Dougal, 'I mean, there's no evidence of this fella hanging about waiting to make his move, and he didn't storm into the shop like some nutter on crack, but he was vicious.'

'Vicious?'

'Aye, the owner took a blow to the head with a lump hammer.'

'A lump hammer?' said Munro. 'So, you've got the weapon?'

'Oh aye. The fella left it behind. Well, not so much left it – he tossed it into the shop on his way out.'

'That's very considerate of him,' said Munro. 'What else?'

'I've scanned the footage from the security camera and…'

'Camera? Singular? You mean he's got just the one?'

'Aye,' said Dougal, 'it's above the door pointing towards the rear of the shop. Anyway, the raid, well, it's all a bit half-hearted.'

'How so?'

'Well, the robber walks in, the owner clocks him; then, quick as a flash, he hits the panic button.'

'And naturally that's when the alarm went off?'

'Correct. Then the robber comes into view, takes a swipe at the owner, and knocks him for a six before walking out.'

'Walking?'

'Aye.'

'He didnae run?'

'No.'

Intrigued by the assailant's detached demeanour after such a wanton act of aggression, Munro, dismissing robbery as a motive, silently pondered alternative reasons for the attack as he gazed blankly towards the car park below.

'The fellow with the hammer,' he said, as if talking to himself. 'Did he actually steal anything?'

'We'll not know for sure until they've done some sort of inventory, boss, but obviously that was his intention.'

'It's not obvious at all,' said Munro.

'I'm not with you.'

'A gentleman walks into a jeweller's shop armed with a carbon steel hammer. Do you not think he'd have smashed a cabinet or two and made off with something even if the alarm was ringing in his ears?'

'Well, maybe.'

'No maybe about it,' said Munro. 'He didnae. And if the owner, as you say, sounded the alarm without even greeting this chap, then you have to ask yourself the question, did he recognise him?'

'Are you saying this was not a robbery at all?'

'I'm saying you have to keep an open mind. It could have been a botched raid, aye, I'll give you that. And it's not beyond the realms of possibility that this fellow simply panicked and lashed out when he heard the alarm. But there could be another reason.'

'Like what?'

'Dear God,' said Munro, 'think, laddie! Perhaps it was something of a personal nature. Perhaps it was a vendetta. Perhaps this jeweller rubbed somebody up the wrong way and it was payback time. Have you run a check on him yet? The owner?'

'Well, no,' said Dougal. 'I mean, he's the victim here and I've been trying to trace the perpetrator.'

'Well, I'd make it your next task if I were you,' said Munro. 'How is he, anyway?'

'Not good, boss. He's in the ICU, completely comatose.'

'There's a surprise. Have you a name?'

'I have,' said Dougal. 'Ross Hunter. Fifty-one years old, married. He's got a big house in Troon, on Southwood Road.'

'So, he's not short of a bob or two?'

'No, quite the opposite.'

'And his wife?' said Munro. 'Has she been informed?'

'Aye. Uniform took her to the hospital this morning. I'll have a chat with her just as soon as I get my act together.'

Munro fastened his tie, grabbed his coat, and headed for the door.

'Leave it to me,' he said. 'You've enough on your plate.'

'Hold on, boss! Uniform might not let you through to see her. No offence, but you've not a got a warrant card anymore, I mean, you're a volunteer.'

'Then you'd best give them a call,' said Munro. 'Tell them I'm on my way. Just don't mention the warrant card.'

Chapter 4

Had he been rifling through a bin bag behind the local supermarket, there is little doubt that Duncan – in his battered, leather car coat, filthy jeans, and tatty woollen watch cap – would have been chased off the premises by over-zealous security guards amidst a torrent of abuse and accusations of theft.

Peggy McClure, astounded that anyone, let alone a respectable, young detective, would choose to dress like a homeless jakey, smiled as she passed round the coffees.

'Are you not warm in that?' she said, nodding towards his coat. 'I mean, it must be twenty degrees, at least.'

'No, no. Not me,' said Duncan. 'I'm as cool as the proverbial cucumber.'

'He's lying,' said West as she sipped her coffee. 'He's probably sweltering under that but he can't take it off, it's like a second skin.'

'One that needs shedding,' said McClure. 'So, have you found anything else yet?'

'Nothing out of the ordinary, and this is the last bag.'

'You sound disappointed.'

'Yeah, right. It's nice to know that the pinnacle of my career as a DI is sifting through other people's tat.'

'Oh, it's not that bad,' said Duncan. 'At least it's just bottles, and boxes, and stuff. It's not as if you're up to your elbows in nappies or garden waste.'

'Even so.'

'Besides, you never know what you might find…'

'That's what I'm afraid of.'

'…a ring maybe? Or an antique?'

'Dream on,' said West. 'Right, I hate to say it, Miss McClure, but the bad news is… we're going to have to go through all of your skips.'

'Good luck with that, they're huge. You'll be here for weeks.'

'Weeks? How many have you got?'

'Eleven or twelve.'

'Twelve!'

'Aye,' said Peggy. 'Let's see now, there's three for glass, one for tins and cans. Then there's plastics, cardboard, textiles, garden, hardcore, oh, and the two walk-ins for furniture and televisions and stuff.'

'Brilliant,' said West with a sigh, 'that's all I need, but we've got no choice. We have to be absolutely certain they haven't been dropping off body parts on a regular basis.'

'So, you think there's more?' said Peggy. 'An arm? Or a leg, maybe?'

'Oh, it's unlikely,' said Duncan. 'I mean, losing a couple of fingers is one thing, losing a couple of limbs is plain careless. We'll be as quick as we can, but it'll probably take a few days.'

'A few days?' said Peggy. 'I'm not entirely sure we can close for that long.'

'You can if I say so,' said West. 'Don't worry, I'll sort it with the council but this place is staying shut for the rest of the day, got that?'

'Aye, no bother. Will it be yourselves doing the checking?'

'God, no. I'll organise a team to come down, they might even start this afternoon. Look on the bright side, you'll get a few days off.'

'Aye, lucky you,' said Duncan. 'You could make a wee holiday of it, you and your partner; take yourselves off to the beach or something.'

'Oh, there is no partner,' said Peggy, 'it's just myself. And Bobby the Bruce.'

'Sorry?'

'My wee doggy. He's a Border.'

'That's smashing! I'm doggy daft, me. Is he here?'

'No, I can't bring him to work, it's too dangerous.'

'So, he's okay being left alone?'

'Aye, of course. It's not for long. I go home for lunch so he gets a wee walk and a squirt, then.'

'I'm glad to hear it,' said Duncan. 'I'm not being funny, but it's not right leaving a dog alone all day, it's not fair.'

'I quite agree, Sergeant. You're quite the softy really, aren't you? Underneath that... soiled exterior.'

'I'll take that as a compliment.'

West took a seat on the bench, pulled off her gloves, and drained her mug.

'Do you mind if we run over a few things?' she said. 'Just to refresh my memory.'

'Aye, no bother. What do you need to know?'

'Well, it was you who found the fingers, right?'

'Aye, it was indeed,' said Peggy. 'Gave me a fair fright too when I realised what they were.'

'I bet it did. And did you look for anything else before you came to us? I mean, did you go rummaging through the other bags, for example?'

'No, no. That was enough for us.'

'Us?'

'Aye. Gordon and me. Gordon Miller, he's my colleague, and a lovely fella he is, too.'

'Is he around?'

'No, he's on his lunch on account of the fact he starts early.'

'When?'

'Six o'clock,' said Peggy.

'And you?'

'Seven-thirty. Eight, maybe.'

'Okay, we might need a word with him later,' said West. 'Tell me, when you arrive for work, do you come through the main gates? Where all the rubbish was dumped?'

'No, we use the entrance round the back.'

'What about the CCTV? Did you sort out a copy for us?'

'Aye, the girls in the office sent it to that email address you gave me, McCrae at something or other.'

'And did you take a look at it yourself?'

'Aye. Well, not me personally,' said Peggy, 'Gordon did. It's standard practice when anything's left at the gates. We try and identify the culprits so the council can issue a fine.'

'And did you?' said West. 'Identify who dumped the bag, I mean?'

'Oh, I wouldn't know, you'd best ask Gordon about that. He didn't say anything, so I'm assuming no.'

West gazed at the rubbish on the ground, stood up, and handed Peggy the empty mug.

'The thing is,' she said, 'why would someone dump a single carrier bag here at the gates? I mean, it would've been easier to toss it in his own bin and then there'd have been no comeback.'

'Perhaps his bin was full,' said Peggy.

'Then he could have chucked it in his neighbour's bin, or used one on the street.'

'Not if he's a greenie,' said Duncan, 'you know, the conscientious, save-the-planet type, and you're forgetting, we don't have bin collections for recyclables here, folk have to drop it off themselves.'

'Even so, it's a bit of an effort, isn't it?'

'Maybe, but there's always the possibility that he didn't actually know what was in the tin.'

'Oh, I never thought of that!' said Peggy. 'You mean, like, someone could've planted them? The fingers? Oh, you're clever, you are. No wonder you're a detective.'

'I'm not clever,' said Duncan, 'I just have a devious mind.'

'Even when you're not working?'

'Good grief,' said West, pulling on her coat, 'I've stumbled into an episode of Blind Date. Miss McClure, we'll be in touch.'

Chapter 5

Despite leaving the Glasgow Royal Infirmary by the front door and not, as he'd predicted, via the mortuary, Munro – still reeling from the trauma of bypass surgery – was tormented, nonetheless, by an unfounded if not irrational fear of hospitals.

Experiencing a mild attack of the jitters as the pervasive stench of chlorine dioxide filled his nostrils, he made his way hurriedly to the ICU and growled at the young, uniformed officer stationed outside a private room.

'I'm after a Ross Hunter,' he said impatiently.

'Oh, you must be Inspector Munro! They told me you were coming. PC Flint, sir.'

'Well, now that we've got the introductions over with, perhaps you'd care to tell me where he is.'

'Sorry. He's in there, sir,' said Flint, nodding over his shoulder. 'But I'm afraid I'm under strict instructions not to let anyone in without the doctor's say-so.'

'Good. And his wife?'

'Just around the corner, sir. She's in the visitors' lounge.'

* * *

Elegantly dressed in a chic two-piece suit, the petite Eileen Hunter, her hair trimmed to a neat, brown bob, sat cross-legged clutching a handbag with the demure sophistication of a Monacan princess.

'Mrs Hunter?' said Munro as he entered the room. 'James Munro.'

'Police?'

'Aye. If it's not a good time, I can always…'

'It's quite alright,' said Hunter. 'Do come in.'

Surprised by the clipped Edinburgh accent, Munro smiled politely and closed the door.

'I'll do my best to keep this brief,' he said, taking a seat. 'I appreciate it cannae be easy for you just now. Silly question, I know, but how are you bearing up?'

'I'm okay, I think. Actually, no. To be perfectly honest, I'm still getting over the shock.'

'Well, I'm not surprised,' said Munro. 'When something like this happens out of the blue, it's only natural that…'

'But that's just it,' said Hunter, 'I was half expecting it.'

'Oh?'

'Being a jeweller, I mean. I just knew that someone, someday, would walk right in and take advantage. I thought I'd be prepared for it, but I'm not. I'm not at all.'

'Aye, it's a terrible state of affairs when a fellow cannae go about his business without fear of attack. Can I fetch you something? A cup of tea perhaps?'

'That's very kind of you, Mr Munro, but I'm fine for now.'

'As you wish. So, is there anything you can tell me about the raid on your shop?'

'Not really,' said Hunter. 'I'm afraid all I know is what I've been told, that somebody went into the shop and smacked poor Ross about the head. Obviously, someone too lazy to take a job.'

'Aye, right enough,' said Munro, 'some folk are always looking for the easy way out. See here, Mrs Hunter, I have to ask you a few questions now but they may seem to be a wee bit personal. Are you okay with that?'

'I don't see why not, but why? Why personal, I mean?'

'Well, I suppose the main reason would be to establish whether or not your husband knew his attacker.'

'Knew his attacker?' said Hunter. 'Forgive me for saying so, but that's a ludicrous idea. Highly unlikely, indeed.'

'Maybe, but it's an avenue we have to tread.'

'Very well. If we must.'

'Good. So, first of all,' said Munro, 'you and your husband, you're happy together?'

'Of course we are. We always have been.'

'And financially speaking, are you okay?'

'I'm sorry?'

'You've no debts hanging over your head? No loans that need repaying?'

'Are you suggesting that this is some sort of an insurance scam?'

'No, no. I simply have to ask the question.'

'Well, you'll be pleased to know,' said Hunter, indignantly, 'that we're quite comfortable, thank you very much. In fact, we're very comfortable, indeed.'

Munro, unsure whether the sudden rise in temperature was due to a faulty thermostat, Hunter's attitude, or an impending relapse, sat back and loosened his tie.

'And your husband Ross, are you aware of any problems on his side of things? With the business, I mean?'

'None. Business is booming, and that's because we don't deal in fashion items, we sell only the best. You'll not find a watch in our shop for less than two thousand pounds.'

'A fool and his money,' said Munro, muttering under his breath.

'I'm sorry?'

'I say, that's probably why you were targeted. Have you had any break-ins before?'

'Never. This is the first.'

Munro leaned forward, clasped his hands beneath his chin, and fixed Hunter with a steely blue gaze.

'Forgive me for asking,' he said, softening his glare with a smile, 'I've no intention of insulting your integrity, but the folk you deal with on the business side of things, suppliers and the like, I take it they're all above board?'

'Why, of course!' said Hunter. 'You'll not find us dealing with anyone but licensed distributors, if not the manufacturers direct.'

'And you can prove that, can you?'

'I beg your pardon?'

'Och, I dinnae mean to sound harsh, Mrs Hunter, especially at a time like this, but I'm simply asking, if we had to go through your books, would everything be in order?'

'Right down to the last penny.'

'Good. Let's change the subject. Tell me about your family.'

'Family? There is no family,' said Hunter. 'It's just Ross and myself.'

'So, no weans? No brothers or sisters? No nieces or nephews?'

Hunter glanced furtively around the room, took a deep breath, and sighed.

'Just the boy,' she said.

'The boy? You've a son?'

Hunter raised her eyebrows and nodded.

'Well, does he have a name? This son of yours?'

'Kieran.'

'That's a fine name,' said Munro. 'And how old is Kieran?'

'I imagine he'll be about fifteen, now.'

'You imagine? Forgive me for saying so, Mrs Hunter, but it sounds as though you've not much interest in the lad. Where is he now?'

'At school,' said Hunter. 'Aberdeen.'

'Aberdeen?'

'Lathallan.'

'So he's a boarder?'

'He is,' said Hunter. 'We don't get to see him much.'

'Och, I can imagine how that feels,' said Munro. 'It must be quite a disappointment.'

'He's the disappointment, Mr Munro. He's not what you'd call academically gifted.'

'I see.'

'But they say he excels at art.'

'Well, that's something to be proud of,' said Munro. 'Even Picasso had to start somewhere.'

'If you say so.'

Munro, irked that anyone could treat their offspring like an unwanted pet, moved on lest his anger get the better of him.

'How about your friends,' he said. 'Are there any jealous types amongst them?'

'I'm not sure I understand.'

'It's not unusual for folk to envy their peers' success, Mrs Hunter; harbour a grudge, even.'

'Our friends are above all that, Mr Munro, and they're all successful in their own right.'

'Well, I'm glad to hear everything's rosy in the land of milk and honey. Tell me, how long have you lived in Troon?'

'Oh, it must be eight or nine years, now,' said Hunter. 'Nine, I think.'

'And before that?'

'Morningside.'

'Oh, very nice. So, what brought you here from Edinburgh?'

'We wanted somewhere quieter. And a house with a garden.'

'Could you not have got that where you were?'

'We might be comfortable, Mr Munro, but we're not millionaires.'

'Fair enough. And what about work? Were you in the same line of business?'

'We were,' said Hunter, shaking her head. 'Fifteen years. I'll not deny it was a bit of an upheaval, but sometimes, one just has to move on.'

'As will I,' said Munro. 'Just one more question and I'll leave you in peace. Is there anyone you might have had a run-in with recently? Yourself or Ross?'

'What do you mean?'

'Oh, I'm not sure exactly, just anyone, anyone at all, that you might have rubbed up the wrong way? A silly, wee argument, perhaps? Or maybe someone tried to tap you for a loan and you knocked them back?'

'Oh, that's utterly vulgar,' said Hunter. 'The very thought of it.'

'I'll take that as a no, then. Look, I hope I've not upset you too much. I know it cannae be easy.'

'It's quite alright, Mr Munro. Water off a duck's back.'

Blaming the cinnamon-spiced apple pie for his sudden bout of indigestion, Munro, pausing by the door, pulled a handkerchief from his pocket, dabbed the beads of perspiration from his forehead, and turned to face Hunter.

'Are you stopping here for the foreseeable?' he said, mustering a sympathetic smile.

'I am,' said Hunter, 'despite the inconvenience.'

'Inconvenience?'

'Aye, we're meant to be flying to Mallorca this evening.'

'I see,' said Munro, smiling with disbelief. 'Well, I'm glad to see you've got your priorities straight, Mrs Hunter. Off on your holidays, were you?'

'It's more than just a holiday, Mr Munro. We're selling our apartment in Santa Ponsa. I thought it was time we upgraded to something more substantial.'

'And what would that be?'

'A villa in Santanyi. It's only the five bedrooms but it will have to do. If we're not there tomorrow to sign the paperwork, then there's every chance we could lose it.'

'Och, I'm sure once you explain your situation they'll be more than understanding.'

'Perhaps,' said Hunter, 'but frankly, if there's no improvement with Ross then I shall have no choice.'

'Well, I cannae blame you for that,' said Munro. 'If I was in your position, I'd cancel the trip as well.'

'Cancel? And let a perfectly good airline ticket go to waste? Oh no, Mr Munro, I'm not cancelling anything.'

Chapter 6

Sceptical of the methods used by criminal psychologists whose conclusions were based purely on hypotheses, DS Dougal McCrae, a traditionalist at heart, believed the key to cornering any suspect lay in the critical analysis of documentary evidence and the studious review of the facts, a process which, fuelled by sugar, often resulted in feelings of extreme lethargy and a thumping headache.

Weary to the point of exhaustion, and frustrated by his failure to establish a motive for the attempted heist on the jewellery store and the lacklustre but nevertheless intimidating hold-ups by the scooter-riding amateurs, he switched off his computers, threw his head back, and held his arms aloft in a gesture of defeat.

'That's me,' he said. 'I need a couple of hours by the loch to clear my head.'

'It's not fish you're needing,' said Duncan, 'it's the love of a good woman. I can fix you up, if you like.'

'You're incorrigible,' said West. 'Besides, you're spoken for, remember?'

'Who said anything about me? It's not an offence to fraternise with members of the opposite sex, you know?'

'It is, as far as you're concerned. Come on, let's call it a day, I'm absolutely starving.'

'I'll second that,' said Duncan. 'I could murder a pint.'

'Did somebody say murder?' said Munro as he trudged through the door. 'Because those stairs will be the death of me.'

West, unable to contain her joy at seeing her mentor back on his feet, leapt from her seat and laughed.

'Jimbo! What the hell are you doing here?'

'It's a shortcut to the cemetery. If I'd any sense, I'd have stayed at home.'

'What?'

'George. He forced me to eat a huge piece of prime sirloin and a bowlful of apple pie.'

'Forced?'

'Well, it would have been rude to refuse,' said Munro. 'He was after a favour.'

'Anything we should know about?'

'Just a few lines on the remarkable achievements of a certain DS who, without my help, will almost certainly be continuing his career in the Outer Hebrides.'

'Thanks, chief,' said Duncan. 'Goes without saying, I appreciate your help.'

'Nonsense, you're as much a part of the team as young Dougal's Irn-Bru; speaking of whom, you're looking awful peaky laddie, have you been injecting the stuff?'

'No, and more's the pity,' said Dougal. 'It's just fatigue; these cases are taking their toll, I'm fair shattered.'

'Right,' said Munro as he took a seat. 'Let's have it.'

'Oh, leave it out,' said West. 'We're all knackered, Jimbo. It's time to shove off.'

'Well, I need to catch my breath, Charlie, so you may as well keep me company while I get my oxygen debt back in the black.'

'I'm not fussed,' said Dougal, 'I'll happily fill you in.'

'Well, what are you waiting for, laddie? Chop, chop, the clock's ticking.'

'Okay, see this fella who robbed the jewellery store?'

'You're sure he robbed them?'

'Well, no!' said Dougal. 'That's just it, I'm not sure he did! But if that was his intention, then why did he not cover his face? Why did he not get in and out as quick as he could?'

'Like I said, perhaps robbery wasnae the motive after all.'

'But that makes things even worse! If you go into a shop to batter some poor fella about the head, for whatever reason, then you don't stroll in like you're browsing for curtains and wander out again!'

'Well, according to his wife…'

'Wife?' said West. 'Is that where you've been? The hospital?'

'Aye,' said Munro. 'I have indeed. You two were out and Dougal had his hands full.'

'So, what's she like?'

'Och, she's all fur coat and no knickers.'

'Sorry?'

'She likes to think she's a blue-blooded toff, but she isnae.'

'So?'

'Well, she cannae think of a reason why anyone would want to hurt her husband and, I have to say, despite her airs and graces, she appears genuine enough.'

'Sounds to me like this Ross Hunter geezer might have a couple of skeletons in the closet.'

'My thoughts exactly,' said Munro. 'You'd do well to run a thorough check on the fellow, and I'll give you a heads-up, they ran a similar business in Edinburgh before they upped sticks and moved here.'

'What do you reckon, chief?' said Duncan. 'Do you think they did a flit?'

'Who knows? According to Eileen Hunter they simply wanted a change of scenery but from where I'm standing, it's a step down the ladder from Morningside, and let's face it, they're not the kind of folk who shop in Poundland. Something's not quite right, but it's up to you to find out what.'

'I'll add it to my list,' said Dougal, 'which isn't getting any shorter.'

'And by the way,' said Munro, 'they've a wean, a young lad by the name of Kieran.'

'That's news to me,' said Duncan. 'Why did uniform not mention it when they picked her up?'

'He's not here, they packed him off to boarding school in Aberdeen. The poor lad never gets to see his own parents. In fact, I'd go so far as to say she's near enough disowned him.'

'Why would anyone do that?'

'There might be several reasons,' said Munro, 'but I fear in this instance it's because he interfered with her social life; speaking of which, she's not the happiest bunny in the world.'

'Well, that's a given,' said Duncan, 'she's probably at her wit's end with worry.'

'Aye, she is, but it's nothing to do with her husband. This wee incident's put the kybosh on her holiday.'

'Holiday?' said West. 'At this time of year?'

'They've a wee place abroad,' said Munro. 'In Santa Ponsa. They're selling it and buying a big villa instead.'

'How the other half live, eh? Alright for some, jetting off to Mallorca whenever they feel like it. I hope it's a flipping time-share.'

'Take that chip off your shoulder, Charlie. You cannae berate hard-working folk for wanting to enjoy themselves. Another twenty years and you could be in the same boat.'

'Bring it on,' said West, keen to uncork a Chianti. 'I can't wait, but knowing my luck my summer retreat will be a bleeding croft on Fair Isle. Come on, if you're not in a hurry to get home, we'll head back to mine. I'll cook.'

'Not so fast!' said Dougal. 'I'm not done yet.'

'What?'

'The lads on the mopeds.'

'For crying out loud! Alright, but make it quick. I'm beginning to feel like I've got worms.'

'I finally got the address of the numpty who paid for his fuel with his bank card. We need to pay him a visit.'

'I'll do that,' said Duncan, 'but not now, I'm dying of thirst.'

'But it's not even the back of six!' said Dougal, 'and he's only…'

'Listen, pal, it's not as if we're looking for an axe murderer; we're looking for some ned with an IQ of 3. I'll go in the morning.'

'If you two have finished discussing your schedule,' said Munro, 'perhaps we could move on.'

'Aye, sorry boss,' said Dougal, 'I'll not keep you long, it's just that I'm having the same problem with these fellas as I am with the loon in the jewellers.'

'How so?'

'A motive. These two lads roll up outside three different locations, start kicking-off with the owners, then leg it when they're chased down the street empty-handed. Not even a bag of sweeties between them. I mean, what on earth are they up to?'

Having spent a lifetime trying to establish the reason behind his wife's predilection for souring the taste of an otherwise perfectly palatable roast dinner with garlic and herbs, or why Americans insisted on diluting a majestic malt with 'rocks' of ice, Munro had become peerlessly adept at determining the motive behind any seemingly irrational action.

He leaned back, clasped his hands behind his head, and closed his eyes as he pondered the conundrum.

'The fellow you've yet to see,' he said, 'the chap at the petrol station. What's his name?'

'Navinder Singh-Gill.'

'That's a novelty,' said Duncan. 'An Indian fella doing hold-ups? I've not heard of that before.'

'These are all his victims,' said Dougal as he handed Munro a sheet of paper. 'They're all nice fellas, I can't see why anyone would want to rob them.'

Munro walked to the window, took his spectacles from his breast pocket, and scanned the list.

'All these names are the same,' he said, raising his eyebrows. 'Are these gentlemen related?'

'Oh, it's unlikely, boss. I mean, it's a common enough name. It's probably just coincidence.'

'Is it?' said Munro. 'Is it, indeed? I think it's time we had a wee quiz.'

'Smashing! We've not had one of those in a while.'

'Here we go,' said West, rolling her eyes. 'I've just lost three stone in weight and you want to play twenty questions?'

'How are you on theology?' said Munro.

'I don't believe this.'

'Your starter for ten. If I said "Goldberg", what would you say?'

Deafened by the ensuing silence, Munro turned to face the room, stared at the three blank faces, and allowed himself a wry smile.

'No? Let's try another. What would you say, if I said "Cohen"?'

Duncan swung his feet onto the desk, folded his arms, and smiled.

'Oh, I see where you're going with this, chief.'

'Do you?'

'Aye, it's obvious.'

'Then let's try another. If I said "Singh-Gill", what would you say?'

'Sikh.'

'And if I said "Khan", what would you say?'

'Muslim.'

'Full marks to the chap from the undergrowth.'

'Sorry,' said West, sighing as she ruffled her hair, 'my blood sugar's dropping, I can't keep up.'

'It's as plain as the nose on your face, Charlie! Think about it!'

'It's not about robbery at all,' said Duncan. 'There's something else going on here, and if I'm not mistaken, it's something to do with religion.'

'Religion?'

'Aye. All the businesses that were targeted; the petrol station, the mini-mart, and the kebab shop, are all run by fellas called "Khan". They're Muslims, but the fellas on the mopeds are Sikhs. Dougal, pal, if I were you, I'd check if they're related after all, and I'll bet you a pint that they are.'

* * *

Without a partner or a spouse to ridicule her housekeeping skills, West, content to languish in a world of organised chaos, used the floor of her apartment as a repository for dirty laundry, the sink as a receptacle for empty wine bottles, and the sofa as a substitute bed when, tired of shouting at the television like a senile old spinster, the trip to the bedroom was too much to handle.

Oblivious to the mismatched socks littering the hallway, she made her way to the dining room, dumped the groceries on the table, and kicked off her boots as Munro, no stranger to the mayhem in which she lived, hung his coat over a chair and glanced towards the kitchen with a distinct look of despair.

'Dear God,' he said, 'I've pulled destitute junkies from hovels that were neater than this. Have you not familiarised yourself with the concept of cleaning yet?'

'It's not as bad as it looks,' said West. 'I'll do it in a minute. First things first, do you want some plonk?'

'Does a fish need water?'

'Are you alright, Jimbo? You're looking a bit peaky.'

'Aye,' said Munro as he began decanting the sink. 'I had a wee turn at the hospital, but I'm fine now.'

'What do you mean, *a wee turn*?'

'It was nothing. A hot flush, that's all.'

'That's all? It's not the bleeding menopause, Jimbo! You should get yourself checked out!'

'Och, calm yourself, lassie! It wasnae me, it was the room. It was far too warm in there.'

'All the same,' said West as she handed him a glass, 'I don't like the sound of it. The last thing I need right now is you croaking on my doorstep.'

'You're all heart.'

'And if you're drinking that, there's no way you're driving home, you can crash here. The spare room's all made up. At least that way I can keep an eye on you. Now, what do you fancy for supper?'

'What do we have?'

'Steak and chips?'

'As much as I love my friend Angus from Aberdeen,' said Munro, 'two in one day would be excessive.'

'How about some chicken, then?'

'Roasted?'

'Curry.'

'Definitely not.'

'In that case,' said West, 'it'll have to be a fry-up. Square sausage, bacon, eggs, beans, black pudding, and a couple of tattie scones; will that do you?'

'Aye, perfect, lassie. Just what the doctor ordered.'

'I doubt that. I doubt that very much.'

* * *

When dining with his belated wife who, like himself, had an appetite politely described as 'healthy', Munro would enjoy devouring his meal, lest it go cold, in complete and utter silence, an experience yet to be repeated in the company of West.

'So, come on then,' she said, 'did you get Duncan's school report sorted out?'

'I did indeed,' said Munro as he dolloped a pool of brown sauce onto his plate. 'I left it with George. Mrs

Elliot will type it up and no doubt embellish it with some well-chosen adjectives.'

'Do you think it will work?'

'I hope for your sake it does, or you'll be joining Duncan on his trip up the creek, and you'll not have a paddle between you.'

'That's what I like about you,' said West. 'You're always so reassuringly optimistic.'

'You know me, Charlie. I'm not happy unless I'm being miserable. So, Laurel and Hardy have their hands full. What are you up to?'

'I have to get my head round this hoo-ha with Fingers McGraw. I mean, I've got his fingers, I just have to find the rest of him. Dougal's checked out the hospitals and the GP surgeries but no-one's seen hide nor hair of him.'

'Maybe he sought treatment farther afield,' said Munro. 'Girvan, or Kirklandside, perhaps?'

'Nope. Been there, done that.'

'What about our friend, Dr McLeod? Has he not come back with anything that might identify this chap?'

'Not yet,' said West. 'I'll give him a bell tomorrow.'

'And that's it?'

'Afraid so. I've got a team going down the recycling centre tomorrow to sift through all the skips, but the fact of the matter is, if they don't come up with something else, we're pretty much scuppered.'

Munro, angered by her somewhat defeatist attitude, pushed his plate to one side and topped up their glasses.

'Forget about the facts, Charlie,' he said sternly, 'and tell me what you think.'

'Alright,' said West. 'My powers of deduction might not be up to Poirot's standards but, judging by the size of the fingers and the state of his fingernails, I'd say he was a well-built labourer with a twenty a day habit who'd just come back from two weeks in Torremolinos. Oh, and whatever sliced them off was bleeding sharp; it made a very clean cut. I reckon it was a cleaver or something.'

'Good, Charlie, that's more like it. Now, dinnae take this the wrong way, but do you not think if some chap was waving a cleaver around he'd have lopped off all four fingers and not just the three?'

'Yeah, you'd have thought so, wouldn't you? Which means whoever did it is either an expert swordsman or there's one left to find.'

'And they were in a can of dog food?'

'Yup. But that doesn't necessarily mean that the culprit, or the victim, owns a dog.'

'No, quite right,' said Munro. 'Perhaps you should be looking for a fellow called Fido, after all.'

Believing something she'd said had rankled Munro enough to drive him to the balcony, West, on the brink of delivering an unsubstantiated apology, gave him a moment alone before joining him outside with two tumblers of whisky.

'Are you alright?' she said as he watched the sun set over the Firth of Clyde. 'You took off a bit sharpish.'

'Aye,' said Munro, swirling the Balvenie around the glass. 'Never better. Your good health.'

'So, what are you thinking about?'

'I was thinking, Charlie, do you not think these two cases might be related?'

'Which two exactly?'

'Our fingerless friend and the jeweller.'

'Nah, don't be daft,' said West. 'Sorry, Jimbo, but I think you're joining the dots and making a scrawl.'

'Is that so, lassie? Is that so?'

'Come on, then. Let's have it.'

'You think this fellow's a smoker, is that right?'

'Yup. Duncan reckons so too. And the nicotine stains are so bad he's probably on roll-ups.'

'And he has a tan?' said Munro, shaking his head. 'I've never seen the attraction myself, lying in the sun, roasting until you're the colour of a barbecued sausage, but some folk enjoy it. Like that Eileen Hunter. I imagine she'd not be happy until she's the colour of a crispy duck.'

'I wouldn't know,' said West. 'I can't remember the last time I was on a beach.'

'You're not listening, Charlie. I said some folk enjoy having a tan. Like Eileen Hunter.'

West, frowning as though she'd been asked to spell "squamous cell carcinoma", glared at Munro and reached for her phone, her eyes widening as the penny dropped.

'Dougal!' she said. 'Sorry mate. Look, I know it's late but I knew you'd be up.'

'No bother, miss. What do you need?'

'Ross Hunter. I need to know if he's got any connections in Spain. Business or otherwise.'

'Spain?'

'That's what I said. Oh, for crying out loud, do I have to spell it out for you? The Hunters have got a place in Santa Ponsa, right? And the fingers in the bag have got a suntan, right?'

'Jeez-oh! Of course! So, you're thinking maybe they've been up to something shady in Spain? That this attack was some kind of a hit after all?'

'Maybe,' said West, draining her glass. 'Just, maybe.'

Chapter 7

Unlike Dougal, Mother Teresa, and the Pope, all of whom shared a common belief that everyone was inherently good, Duncan – unable to heal the psychological scars of a misspent youth – was cynically suspicious of every Tom, Dick, and Harry he met.

Alone in the office with his feet on the desk and a computer in his lap, he sat sipping coffee whilst browsing the internet for every snippet of information he could find on the flirty, and inexplicably single, Peggy McClure, barely flinching as West breezed through the door.

'Bloody hell,' she said, 'don't tell me you slept here.'

'Very good.'

'Then, why so early?'

'I've work to do.'

'Carry on like this and you'll be bored out of your skull when you get to Benbecula.'

'I'll have plenty to keep me busy,' said Duncan. 'Especially with you in the spare room.'

'Touché,' said West as she flicked on the kettle. 'Fancy a brew?'

'No, you're alright, thanks. Where's the chief?'

'Bringing up the rear with a couple of toasties.'

'Oh, he'll catch Dougal then. He's down there now.'

'So, what dragged you from your bed at this hour?'

'Peggy McClure.'

'You sly old dog!' said West. 'Don't tell me you and she…'

'Away!' said Duncan. 'She's old enough to be my mother! I'm simply trying to find out what she's been up to.'

'God, you don't trust anyone, do you?'

'No, I do not. If you'd lived my life, you'd know what it's like to be let down.'

'Oh, spare me the heartache!' said West. 'At least your fiancé wasn't doing the dirty behind your back while you were planning a wedding.'

'Oh, aye. Sorry. I forgot about that.'

'No worries. It's all character building, right? So, why the interest?'

'Well, she might be getting on,' said Duncan, 'but she's a good-looking lassie, I'll give her that.'

'So?'

'So, why is she single?'

'Maybe she's not the marrying kind,' said West. 'Just like me.'

'Aye, maybe. But she also owns a dog. And our fingers were found in a tin of dog food.'

'It's a Border Terrier!' said West. 'Hardly the Hound of the Baskervilles now, is it?'

'Size isn't everything,' said Duncan, with a smirk. 'Terriers are renowned for getting their teeth stuck into anything, and let's face it, any dog can be trained to attack, that's why Staffies get such a bad rap, normally because the training methods used by the owners are tantamount to abuse.'

'Fair enough,' said West, 'but unless she's trained it to handle a meat cleaver, I think you're barking up the wrong tree.'

Dressed like an Italian preppy in his neatly pressed chinos and navy-blue polo shirt, Dougal, laden with two brown carrier bags, wandered casually into the office as though he'd just returned from a morning's shopping on Via Montenapoleone.

'You took your time,' said Duncan, 'I'm starving.'

'I got held up. Some doddery old fella needed a hand up the stairs.'

'I'll help you down them in a minute,' said Munro as he strolled through the door. 'Duncan, are you okay?'

'Aye, not bad, chief. You're looking well.'

'I feel it too, and it's all down to a good, healthy diet. You should try it yourself, sometime.'

'I'll bear it in mind.'

'How are you getting on with the Indian fellow on the scooter?'

'I'm away to see him soon,' said Duncan. 'I've just been doing some digging on that Peggy McClure.'

'Sorry, you'll have to refresh my memory.'

'The lassie from the recycling centre.'

'Of course it is.'

'I think Duncan's got a crush on her,' said West.

'Not me, but I think the chief might be interested.'

'How so?' said Munro.

'She's a looker. A bit younger than yourself, but that's not uncommon.'

'See this ring?' said Munro, smiling as he raised his hand. 'It means I'm still married, whether she's around or not. Now then, Charlie, if it's not too much trouble, a cup of tea to go with my aspirin wouldnae go amiss.'

'Coming up.'

'So, did you find anything?' said Dougal. 'On Miss McClure?'

'Nothing that'll put her in Broadmoor, but guess what she did before she started working for the council.'

'Taxidermist?'

'Not quite,' said Duncan. 'She was a pupil support teacher.'

'Is that so?' said Munro as he tore into a bacon roll. 'That's a commendable occupation. Vocational, almost. I wonder what possessed her to give it up?'

'Probably stress,' said West. 'I mean, it can't be easy dealing with kids who are struggling, every day of your life.'

'Right enough,' said Duncan, 'hats off to the woman for doing it for as long as she did. Right, that's me away. What are you two up to?'

'Well, as it's such a nice day, I thought Jimbo and I would pay McLeod a visit.'

'You're having a day out, you mean?'

'It's work.'

'I'd not bother if I were you, miss,' said Dougal. 'He's on his way to Crosshouse for a post-mortem. He's going to drop by on the way.'

'That's even better,' said West, 'it means we can eat our breakfast in peace.'

'It also means you've time to take a look at this.'

'What is it?'

Dougal pulled the blinds and turned his computer to face them as Munro, likening the experience to a matinee performance at the old Regal Cinema on Shakespeare Street, sat back and slurped his tea.

'This,' said Dougal, 'is the overnight footage from the recycling centre. Now, it's a few hours long so I'm going to run it on fast forward, okay? Keep your eyes peeled and you'll see all manner of folk turning up in the dead of night to dump their crap by the gates.'

Munro, fascinated more by the nocturnal activity of an urban fox than the fly-tippers oblivious to the security cameras, sat glued to the screen until Dougal finally pressed pause.

'Well,' he said, 'it's not as exciting as *Destry Rides Again*, but it's entertaining all the same.'

'There's just a couple of seconds to go,' said Dougal as he resumed play. 'Okay, see here, that's Miss McClure come to open the gates.'

'Is that it?' said West. 'Well, they won't be making a sequel, that's for sure.'

Dougal stared at West and raised his eyebrows.

'What?' she said. 'Have I missed something?'

'Put it this way, miss. If this was an interview, I'm really not sure you'd get the job.'

'What?'

'The blue carrier bag with the tin of dog food. It's not there.'

Munro, beaming as though he'd just discovered that the main feature was to be followed by a cartoon, drained his cup and chuckled to himself.

'He's right, Charlie,' he said. 'I'd not give you the job either.'

'This is unbelievable,' said West, huffing as she grabbed her coat. 'Right, come on Jimbo, we need to pick up McClure.'

Seething at Peggy McClure's carefully edited version of events surrounding the discovery of the bag, West, her face flushed with embarrassment, was agitated even further by the sudden appearance of Andy McLeod.

'This is all I need,' she said, rolling her eyes.

'If it's a bad time I can always come back, but you'll not see me until next week.'

'No, it's alright,' said West, 'you'd better come in.'

'Good. I'll not keep you long,' said McLeod. 'I'm running late and I don't like my stiffs going limp on me, if you get what I mean.'

McLeod eased his willowy frame into a chair, nodded politely at Munro, and scratched his coppery beard.

'How are you feeling, James?' he said. 'Still firing on all cylinders?'

'Well, I'm not ready for a marathon just yet,' said Munro, 'but I've no complaints so far.'

'I'm glad to hear it, and listen, I know how you feel about doctors so if you're worried about anything, you know you can give me a call. Anytime.'

'Much appreciated, Andy. I'll bear it in mind.'

'So, Charlie. You're looking well, if not a wee bit harassed.'

'You don't know the half of it,' said West. 'I feel like overdosing on Prozac.'

'You need to relax more,' said McLeod. 'You should try some mindfulness, or yoga, or meditation, maybe.'

'Are you having a laugh?'

'Or a night out. How about that wee drink you've been promising?'

'You couldn't keep up,' said West. 'Besides, I've got too much on at the moment. So, what's the deal?'

'I've some news,' said McLeod, 'about the fingers you asked me to look at.'

'Thank God for that!' said West, her mood lightening. 'As it happens, I've been thinking about them too, and I might just be one step ahead of you.'

'Enlighten me.'

'Right, when we first clapped eyes on them, I instantly assumed, because of the colour, that the geezer who lost them had just been on holiday, right?'

'Okay.'

'But thanks to some blinding input from Jimbo here, I'm now thinking he doesn't have a tan at all. I'm thinking that it's his natural skin colour.'

'Well, I've got to hand it to you, Charlie,' said McLeod with a grin, 'you're on the money there.'

'Okay, so I'm thinking he's probably Spanish.'

'No, no. Sorry. You've just lost a few quid.'

'Alright, Portuguese, then.'

'You're into overdraft.'

'Italian?'

'Your thinking's right,' said McLeod, 'but you're on the wrong continent, that's all.'

'Come again?'

'See here, Charlie, I can't be absolutely certain about everything, I mean, three fingers, it's not much to go on, so I can only guess that whoever parted company with those fingers is *probably* a male, and I can only *estimate* his age, which I'd put at around twenty to twenty-five. But I can tell you one thing without a shadow of a doubt, he's *definitely* an IC4.'

'IC4? You mean he's Asian?'

'To be precise,' said Munro, 'it means he's from the Indian subcontinent, which could be any number of countries. India, for example, or Pakistan, or Bangladesh, or Nepal, or…'

'Yeah, alright,' said West, 'I get the picture. Unfortunately for you, it also means your theory that they're related to the heist on the jewellers goes out the window.'

'It was only a theory, lassie. And if anything, by a process of elimination, it means they're more likely to be connected to the chaps terrorising folk on their mopeds.'

'Those idiots? Oh, for God's sake, they can't even nick a tank of petrol. I hardly think they'd be up to chopping someone's hand off.'

Chapter 8

Away from the hustle and bustle of the town centre, Wheatfield Road, with its views across Low Green and the esplanade to the Firth of Clyde and beyond, was a quiet residential street lined with impressive sandstone villas just a stone's throw from the beach.

A young girl dressed in blue jeans and a bright yellow tee shirt, wary of folk offering to repave the drive or replace the guttering for the price of a brand new 4x4, peered cautiously from behind the barely-open door and called to Duncan as he made his way slowly up the path.

'No thanks,' she said. 'Try next door.'

'Sorry?'

'Whatever it is you're peddling, we don't need it.'

'Actually,' said Duncan, 'I was after Nav.'

'Navinder?'

'Aye.'

'He's not here. He's working.'

'And you are?'

'None of your business.'

Duncan flashed a grin and pulled his warrant card from his back pocket.

'Oh dear,' she said. 'Sorry. I'm Meena, his sister.'

* * *

Meena Singh-Gill, a twenty-one-year-old undergraduate with aspirations of writing earth-shattering exposés as one of Caledonia's finest investigative journalists, opened the door and smiled.

'Has something happened?' she said. 'Is he in some kind of bother?'

'No, no. I'd just like a wee chat, do you know where...'

Interrupted by the sound of a moped in desperate need of a new exhaust, Duncan turned to see a young man sporting skinny jeans, trendy trainers, and an open-face helmet striding towards them.

As a millennial who shunned the teachings of science and the theory of evolution in favour of veganism and gender fluidity, Ash Singh-Gill, who'd described himself as a 'social media influencer' on every one of his failed job applications was, much to his father's chagrin, not in the least bit religious, had no interest in cricket, and preferred to spend his spare time protesting about cultural appropriation rather than helping with the family business.

'Alright?' he said, frostily. 'Can I help you?'

Duncan cocked a smile and nodded towards the bike.

'Nice wheels,' he said. 'Have you had it long?'

'No. And it's a pile of crap.'

'You must have got it cheap, then.'

'I've not bought it,' said Ash. 'I borrowed it.'

'Who from?'

'A pal. What's it to you?'

'I was just wondering,' said Duncan, 'this pal of yours, does he happen to be a delivery driver, by any chance?'

'I don't know. Aye. Maybe.'

'You should tell him his number plate's missing.'

'Okay, that's plenty,' said Ash, 'it's time you left.'

'Ash!' said Meena, cringing. 'He's a policeman!'

'DS Reid,' said Duncan. 'Mind if I have a word?'

Ash removed his helmet, ran a hand through his gelled quiff, and smiled smugly.

'As it happens,' he said, 'I do. I mind a lot. I don't have to talk to you at all. I know my rights.'

'So do I,' said Duncan, 'so we could either go inside, or we could do this down the station.'

'Are you joking me? The station? And what exactly are you going to nick me for?'

'Theft of a motor vehicle.'

'Dream on.'

'What's your name again?'

'Ashar.'

'Good. Ashar Singh-Gill, I'm arresting you on suspicion of…'

'Ash!' said Meena, trying not to shout. 'Grow up and get inside!'

* * *

Overawed by the voluminous hallway and imposing oak staircase, Duncan followed them to the lounge and paused momentarily to gawp at the parquet flooring, the marble fireplace, and the framed paintings of mountainous landscapes adorning the wood-panelled walls, while Ash sprawled himself across a humungous four-seater Chesterfield sofa.

'Are you okay?' said Meena. 'You look a bit lost.'

'Oh, aye,' said Duncan. 'I just wasn't expecting this, that's all. It's smashing, like a stately home. I feel like I should've come in the back door.'

'That's Bapu, for you. Delusions of grandeur.'

'Sorry, hen. Bap who?'

'Bapu. It means "father". So, can I get you something? A cold drink, maybe? We've got juice or cola.'

'Aye, thanks very much. I'll take a juice, please.'

'You can take a pew, too,' said Ash. 'You're making the place look untidy.'

Duncan sunk into a deep, leather armchair, leaned back, and crossed his legs.

'I could get used to this,' he said. 'Oh, and by the way, Mr Singh-Gill, I'd appreciate it if you didn't play with your phone while we talk.'

'You talk,' said Ash, facetiously. 'I'll listen.'

'That's not how it works,' said Duncan. 'I'm going to ask some questions, and you're going to answer them. Now, where's Navinder?'

'At the restaurant.'

'Is it not a bit early for lunch?'

'He's not eating, he's working. It's our restaurant.'

'So, you've a family business?'

'Aye, the Punjabi Grill,' said Ash. 'On Carrick Street.'

'And your folks work there, too? Your parents, I mean?'

'Work there? They're never out of the place. They're the chefs.'

'And how's it doing?'

'Aye, good as ever, and that's because folk appreciate decent, home-cooked food.'

'I'll have to swing by,' said Duncan. 'I love a good curry, me. Not too hot mind, I'm more of a korma man, myself.'

'Well, don't go expecting any freebies,' said Ash. 'I wouldn't want to be accused of bribing a police officer.'

'No. That would never do. So, about the scooter.'

'What about it?'

'Why did you steal it?'

'I didn't steal it. I found it.'

'Lying in the street?'

'Aye.'

'With the keys in the ignition?'

'Aye.'

'You know the fella you nicked it off had to walk home?'

'He was overweight,' said Ash. 'I did him a favour.'

Had the gentleman lying on the sofa been a serial offender suspected of ABH, his prowess at verbal ping-pong would have been enough to make Duncan reach for his cuffs but, coming from a nine stone teen who identified with Narcissus, he couldn't help but smile.

'Tell me, Ash,' he said, 'have you got a motor yourself?'

'No. I've not passed my test.'

'What about Nav?'

'No. He's not passed it either.'

'So, how do you get around?'

'Taxi.'

'Taxi? So, you're not strapped for cash, then?'

'No way!' said Ash. 'We're minted.'

'Then why,' said Duncan, 'would two young fellas like yourselves want to hold up a petrol station? Or a mini-mart? Or a kebab shop?'

Ash dropped his phone and glanced sheepishly around the room.

'We weren't robbing them,' he said.

'No? What then?'

'I can't say.'

Meena, fulfilling her role as hostess, returned to the room, handed Duncan an ice-cold glass of orange juice, and tucked a tress of jet-black hair behind her ear as she perched on the arm of the sofa.

'Are you hungry?' she said. 'I've a few samosas in the fridge if you're feeling peckish.'

'This is not a hotel,' said Ash. 'I'm sure he's had his breakfast.'

'You're alright, hen,' said Duncan, raising his glass. 'The juice is fine.'

'So, are you going to let me in on the secret, Sergeant? Are you going to tell me what these two tearaways have been up to?'

'I'd love to,' said Duncan, 'but your brother, here, appears to have lost his tongue.'

'That's not like him,' said Meena, 'he's usually such a motor-mouth. Ash, the sooner you answer the sergeant's questions, the sooner he can go.'

56

Ash sat up, took a deep breath, and hung his head.

'Go upstairs,' he said. 'We'll be done in a bit.'

'Upstairs yourself! I'm not a child anymore.'

'Meena! I said go upstairs! And close the door on your way out.'

Duncan locked eyes with Ash and sipped his juice.

'You do know she's probably listening at the door, don't you?'

'Aye. Probably.'

'So, what's the story? What's your beef with the Khans?'

Ash glared across the room, a look of utter bewilderment smeared across his face.

'How do you know about the Khans?' he said.

'I'm a police officer,' said Duncan. 'I know things you've not even learned yet. And I know the Khans own the shops you tried to rob.'

'I told you. We weren't on the rob.'

'So, what then? Were you threatening them? Is there some kind of business rivalry going on here?'

Ash rubbed his dry lips with the palm of his hand and stared at Duncan from beneath a furrowed brow.

'Come on, pal,' said Duncan, 'the meter's ticking. I don't have all day.'

'Okay,' said Ash, 'but if I tell you, it goes no further. No investigations, no going to court, no nothing. If my folks found out, it'd kill them.'

'We'll see. On you go.'

'Tarif Khan.'

'Which one's he?'

'The son.'

'What about him?'

'He and Meena, he…'

'Oh, I get it,' said Duncan, 'is this some kind of religious thing? The fact that you're a Sikh and the Khans are Muslim, is that why…'

'It's got nothing to do with religion!' said Ash, growling from behind gritted teeth. 'I couldn't give a stuff if they were Buddhist Rastafarians! Tarif Khan raped my sister!'

In a brief but varied career, Duncan – hardened to the point of emotional detachment – had taken the comatose junkies, deranged drunks, and even the occasional rotting corpse, in his stride but any case of physical or emotional abuse directed towards the female of the species was guaranteed to raise his hackles.

'When did this happen?' he said softly.

'About three weeks ago.'

'Three weeks?'

'Aye. We only found out a few days ago. Meena, she's not been out of the house, she's not been to college, she's not even been to the shops. We knew something was up but she kept denying it until Nav lost it with her and she cracked.'

'Okay, see here, Ash, my main concern right now is for Meena's health. Has she seen a doctor?'

'No.'

'She needs to. As soon as possible.'

'She'll not go.'

'She will,' said Duncan. 'You leave it to me.'

'No, no,' said Ash, raising his hands. 'She's been through enough, I'll not have you grilling her under a spotlight.'

'Listen, she already knows we're talking about her, she's on the other side of that door, so just calm down, okay? Now, have you reported this to the police?'

'What do you think?'

'Why not?'

'Take your pick. Embarrassment. Shame. Guilt.'

Duncan drained his glass, set it on the table and hauled himself from the chair.

'Listen, Ash,' he said, 'I appreciate your honesty, pal, but you can't go round dishing out vigilante justice just because your sister refuses to go to the police. You'll end up in more trouble than Tarif Khan.'

'I'll take my chances.'

'No, you will not. Okay, I need an address for this Tarif fella, then I need a word with Meena.'

'No, you're not putting her through the…'

Ash's words tailed off as Meena entered the room and cast a half-hearted smile at Duncan.

'It's alright, Ash,' she said. 'You can go.'

Meena waited for the door to close, buried herself in the corner of the sofa, and pulled her knees to her chest.

'Are you okay to talk about this?' said Duncan. 'I could get a female officer if you'd prefer, someone who's trained to…'

'No, you're alright. To be honest, I've been wanting to talk about it for a while but they're so protective they won't let me out of their sight.'

'Navinder and Ash?'

'Aye.'

'Well, it's not a bad thing. They're just looking out for you. Okay, in your own time, Meena, there's no rush. Take as long as you like.'

Chapter 9

Apart from an embarrassing episode at the local DIY store where, at her father's behest, she'd waited patiently for a left-handed screwdriver, some bubbles for a spirit level, and five litres of tartan paint, West did not consider herself to be gullible, nor did she enjoy being taken for a ride.

Hurtling along Heathfield Road in the draughty Defender with her brunette locks billowing about her head, she turned to Munro and scowled.

'I cannae see why you're so upset, Charlie,' he said, winding up the window. 'She's only having a day off.'

'Day off, my backside! It's a bit of a coincidence, isn't it?'

'What is?'

'Peggy bleeding McClure! Disappearing like that!'

'Och, she's not disappeared! You told me yourself that the plant was to remain closed until the SOCOs have finished sifting through the skips. That's why she's not there.'

'Oh, wake up, Jimbo! I've got a bad vibe about this, and I don't like being taken for a mug either. It's as simple as that!'

'Then we'd best stop at the corner shop before we reach her house.'

'Why?'

'Because you'll be needing some tissues,' said Munro, 'to wipe the egg from your face.'

* * *

Disheartened by West's complete disregard for doorstep etiquette, Munro stood back and winced as she hammered the door with the side of her fist and yelled through the letterbox.

'For God's sake!' said Peggy. 'Could you not use the bell? You're scaring the dog half to death!'

'You'll have to forgive her,' said Munro with a disarming smile, 'her medication's wearing off. Can we come in?'

Standing with her back to the window, West slipped her hands into her pockets, shrugged her shoulders, and smiled apologetically.

'Sorry about that,' she said, 'it's been one of those mornings.'

'Oh, you're alright,' said Peggy. 'It happens to the best of us. Why don't you sit yourselves down?'

'Cheers. This is my colleague, by the way. James Munro.'

Unaccustomed as he was to the unconditional love of a canine companion, Munro, cautious at first, beamed as a small Border Terrier leapt to the sofa and snuggled into his lap.

'Well, well, well,' he said as he tentatively stroked its head. 'And who do we have here?'

'That's Bobby the Bruce,' said Peggy. 'He obviously likes you, Mr Munro. What kind do you have?'

'Me? Oh, I've not got one, Miss McClure. Why do you ask?'

'Well, only because nine times out of ten, dogs are attracted to strangers because they can smell another mutt.'

'I see,' said Munro, taking the statement as an affront to his personal hygiene. 'Well, I suggest in this instance we put it down to animal magnetism and move on. What do you say?'

'The last time we met,' said West, doing her best to suppress a grin, 'you told me your mate at the recycling centre went through the footage from the security cameras. Is that right?'

'Gordon, aye. He will have done.'

'Well, so did we. And guess what? Nobody, and I mean absolutely nobody, dumped a blue, plastic carrier bag outside the gates.'

'I know,' said Peggy. 'It was in a bin bag. One of those big black bin bags with the tie-handles.'

'Oh, for God's sake!' said West. 'Why the hell didn't you say so?'

'It never came up.'

'You didn't mention it to DS Reid when he questioned you?'

'No, why would I? I found that stinking can of dog food in the blue bag, so that's what I brought you!'

'And you did the right thing,' said Munro, patting the dog, 'and for that we're grateful. Very grateful indeed, but tell me, Miss McClure, was there anything else in the bag? Anything you might have removed by any chance?'

'No, no. We've not taken anything out, you got the lot. The tin, the fingers, and some of that blue kitchen roll.'

'Okay,' said West, 'what about the black bin bag? Can you remember what was in that?'

'Oh, I never looked, I came straight to you. Gordon would have gone through it, though.'

'Where can we find him?'

'Well, he'll not be at work. At home, perhaps?'

'Do you have a number?'

* * *

West, on the verge of blowing a fuse, stepped outside, took a deep breath and, shielding her eyes from the glare of the sun, leant against the bonnet of the Defender, and dialled.

'Gordon Miller?'

'Aye. Who's this?'

'We've not met. DI West. I'm with your mate, Peggy McClure.'

'Oh aye, very good. Is this about the wee tin of hot dogs?'

'Yeah, listen. She says the blue bag you found them in was inside a black bin liner, is that right?'

'Aye, spot on.'

'And she also says it was up to you to go through the bin liner to try and find out who'd dumped it.'

'All part of the job.'

'And what did you find?'

'Well, there wasn't a head, or a couple of feet, if that's what you're after, but there was enough to issue a fine to the restaurant.'

'Hold on, how do you know it's a restaurant?'

'Because,' said Miller, 'folk are often stupid enough to leave a paper trail. There were loads of empty beer bottles, twenty-four to be exact. Cobra. Some takeaway menus, and an order pad with their name and address on it.'

'Blinding!' said West. 'Have you still got it?'

'Oh aye, of course, it's normal procedure. We take a wee photo of anything incriminating we find, then bag it and file it away.'

'Christ, you're worse than CSI.'

'I'm not happy about it myself,' said Miller. 'The way I see it, if folk have dumped their waste outside the gates, then at least they've made the effort. I see no reason for them to be persecuted.'

'Fair enough,' said West. 'Listen, I need to get my hands on that stuff; any chance you could leave it in the office at the recycling centre and I'll pick it up when I get a chance?'

'Aye, no bother; give me twenty minutes, at least.'

'Perfect. So, are you going to tell me who the culprits are, or are you keeping it to yourself?'

'It's a place on Carrick Street called the Punjabi Grill.'

* * *

As someone who dissected the news for articles based on science, history, and nature, as opposed to those which focused on politics, current affairs, or minor celebrities with surgically-enhanced assets, Munro was well aware of the psychological benefits of a therapy dog for those suffering with anxiety disorders, patients in palliative care, and the unfortunate few undergoing a process of rehabilitation, but to experience first-hand the comfort of a mutually beneficial tummy rub was a unique if not wholly satisfying sensation.

Conscious of what could only be described as a significant lowering of his BP, he heaved a contented sigh and nodded approvingly at the densely-packed bookshelves of McClure's modest lounge.

'I must say, you're quite the scholar, Miss McClure. You're very well read by the looks of it.'

'Oh, don't be fooled,' said Peggy, 'you'll not find Tolstoy or Solzhenitsyn up there. It's mainly boring stuff on counselling and cognitive development.'

'Is that something to do with your previous occupation? I don't mean to pry, but were you not in the teaching profession?'

'Not quite. I was what you call a Learning Support Worker.'

'It must have been very rewarding.'

'That's one word for it.'

'And another would be?'

'Tiring. Stressful. Taxing. It's hard not to become attached to the kids when you're trying to figure out what's holding them back.'

'Aye, that must have been quite a burden,' said Munro, 'emotionally, I mean.'

'It was, and I'm afraid I simply couldn't deal with it anymore. I had to start thinking about me, and my own health.'

'Well, I'll not blame you for that. So, what made you choose to work at the recycling plant?'

'I've really no idea,' said Peggy. 'I suppose I liked the idea of doing something manual, you know, something where I didn't have to think about other folk. And I liked the idea of being outdoors all the time.'

'I get the distinct impression you're enjoying the change.'

'Better than that,' said Peggy, 'I'm loving it. In fact, I couldn't be happier. I can sleep at night, I don't feel obligated to work through my lunch hour, and when we close for the day, that's it, all I have to worry about is what's on the telly.'

Cringing at the sound of the front door slamming shut, Munro, wary of disturbing the dozing dog, attempted to stand as West blundered into the room.

'Let's go!' she said excitedly. 'We've got a lead. Apologies again, Miss McClure, and thanks for your time.'

'You're welcome,' said Peggy as Bobby the Bruce followed Munro down the hall. 'Oh, that's loyalty for you. If you ever fancy dog-sitting, Mr Munro, just give me a call.'

Chapter 10

Apart from a fleeting interruption by a flustered DCI Elliot, Dougal, happiest when left to his own devices, was enjoying the solitude of an empty office when the sound of raised voices along the corridor caused his cheeks to billow with a despondent sigh.

'What's up with you?' said West. 'Time of the month?'

'Can you not see he's busy?' said Munro. 'Leave the lad in peace.'

'Well, pardon me for caring. Before I forget, did you get anywhere with tracing that motor from the smash and grab?'

'Give me a chance,' said Dougal, 'I've no make, no model, and only half the registration. I'm doing my best.'

'Alright, keep your hair on. Any tea on the go?'

'Tea? Is it not time for lunch?'

'Now that you mention it, yup, it certainly is.'

'Well, don't let me keep you.'

'God, you're a right little ray of sunshine, you are. Here,' said West as she tossed him a small, sealed pouch, 'we got this from the recycling centre. It belongs to a place called the Punjabi Grill.'

Dougal, miffed that yet another distraction threatened to keep him from his work, rolled his eyes as Duncan, looking as though he'd been on the receiving end of a lengthy confession at the local church, sauntered into the office.

'Punjabi Grill?' he said. 'What's happening there?'

'We found one of their order pads at the recycling centre,' said West, 'and it just happened to be in the same bag as those festering fingers, which means, one way or another, someone at the restaurant is mixed up in this.'

'Well,' said Duncan as he slumped to his seat, 'I have to say, this is all coming together in a way that's liable to fall apart at the seams any second now.'

'Come on then, let's have it, but make it snappy. I need to eat.'

Duncan glanced at West and scratched the stubble on his chin.

'The Punjabi Grill,' he said, 'it's owned by the Singh-Gills.'

West, fearful that lunch was about to become high tea, snatched a packet of digestives from the cupboard and sat down.

'Alright,' she said. 'What have you got?'

'They've two sons, Navinder and Ashar, who, as we know, were responsible for the raids on the shops owned by the Khans.'

'So, they've admitted it?' said West. 'Even stealing the moped?'

'As good as, aye.'

'Well, aren't you going to nick them?'

'Not just yet,' said Duncan. 'I think we need to keep them on-side for now.'

'Why?'

'Because they weren't on the rob, they were after a fella called Tarif Khan. See here, miss, Nav and Ash have a sister, Meena. She and this Tarif fella were sort of... involved.'

'Oh, I knew it,' said Dougal, 'here we go. Did you know that the number one reason for the majority of conflicts in the world is religion?'

'Aye, I did,' said Duncan, 'but this has nothing to do with religion.'

Detecting an almost pitiful tone to his voice, Munro loosened his tie, leaned forward, and stared solemnly across the table.

'This is not some kind of a jihad, is it, laddie? I get the distinct impression that there's something more serious going on here.'

'Right enough, chief. It appears Meena Singh-Gill was attacked by Tarif Khan, and when I say attacked, I mean...'

'You mean raped?' said West. 'Bleeding low-life scum!'

'And you're sure about this?' said Munro. 'I mean, it's not just some yarn these chaps have spun you to defend their actions?'

'No, no. I'm positive. I had a long chat with Meena. In private. She's given me the time, and the date, and the location.'

'And, of course, they've not reported it to the police, have they?'

'No,' said Duncan, 'and they're not likely to either. She's not even told her parents, but I have convinced her to see a doctor, for her own sake.'

'Seeing a doctor's no good,' said West. 'Can't you persuade her to see an FME?'

'There's no way she's going to let a forensic medical examiner prod away down there. She'll not even see her own GP; she's going to the Gatehouse clinic, instead.'

'Alright,' said West, 'how do you want to play this? It's your call.'

'I'm away to see this Khan fella now, and if he's wearing fingerless mittens then it stands to reason that Ash and Navinder are the ones behind it. To be honest, if it is him, then he's lucky it's just his fingers he lost.'

'That's all well and good,' said West, 'but if Meena's refusing to file a charge against him, we're stuffed. What do we do then?'

'I think our best bet is to come down heavy on him. If he thinks Meena *has* filed a charge, then maybe we'll get a confession.'

'In that case you'd better bring him in. If this Tarif bloke is our ham-fisted friend, we're going to need a swab. Dougal, I want uniform and SOCOs at the restaurant but give me an hour. I need to have a chat with the owners before I shut them down, if they haven't been too heavy handed with the bleach, we might get a trace of Tarif's blood about the place.'

'No bother,' said Dougal. 'Leave it with me.'

'Right, come on, Jimbo; if we're lucky, we might be able to cadge a bite to eat before I kick them out.'

'You're on your own there, Charlie,' said Munro. 'I'm not one for foreign food, as well you know.'

'Oh, come on, you'll enjoy it.'

'Och, I've no doubt my mouth might approve, lassie, but my tummy willnae. No, no, you go and enjoy yourself. I'll share a couple of cheese toasties with young Dougal, here.'

* * *

Like a weary host closing the door on the last of his lingering guests, Dougal – glad to see the back of Duncan and West – returned to his desk and continued to pick his way through the list of white hatchbacks registered with the DVLA while Munro, as happy as a kid with a colouring book, sat silently scrolling through the dozens of dogs up for adoption on the rescue centre website.

Chapter 11

Looking more like the international headquarters of a global electronics giant than a respected seat of learning, the University of the West of Scotland, located on the north bank of the River Ayr, was a sprawling, state-of-the-art affair offering more courses than a taster menu at a Michelin-starred restaurant.

Suspecting the swarthy figure swanning through the main reception hall to be a dealer, a jakey, or an opportunistic thief, the middle-aged lady behind the desk stood abruptly, donned her gold-framed spectacles, and raised her hand like a deluded Canute.

'Can I help you?' she said, her voice quavering.

'Aye, you probably can,' said Duncan, waving his warrant card. 'Detective Sergeant Reid.'

'Oh. I do apologise. It's just that, the way you're dressed, no offence but...'

'Underfunding, hen. We've simply not got enough uniforms to go around at the moment.'

'I see.'

'I'm looking for one of your students,' said Duncan. 'A fella by the name of Khan. Tarif Khan.'

'Oh, dear, is he in some kind of bother?'

'Not necessarily.'

'Drugs, I imagine. They're all at it. Well, let's see if we can't find him for you. Would you happen to know what he's studying?'

'Aye. Journalism.'

'Okey dokey,' said the lady, tapping away at her keyboard. 'Well, according to the schedule there was just the one lecture today and that was this morning, so perhaps you'll find him in his room.'

'And where would that be?'

'Past the car parks at the end of the avenue. I'll get someone to show you. Lizzie!'

A young girl seated at the far end of the desk, who'd shown not the slightest piece of interest in the conversation, closed her magazine, zipped-up her tracksuit, and sprang to her feet wearing a smile as genuine as a sommelier serving a cheap, house red.

'Hello there!' she said. 'I'm Lizzie, the student rep! How can I help you today?'

'Lizzie, kindly escort this gentleman to the residents' block. Room 173, if you don't mind.'

'No bother! Follow me!'

'Just a moment,' said Duncan. 'Sorry, hen, but do you not have some sort of a pass key or something? I need to take a look inside his room, even if he's not there.'

'We have a universal key,' said the lady, removing her glasses, 'but I can't let you in without a warrant, that would be a breach of the law.'

Duncan flashed her a cheeky grin, pulled an envelope from his jacket, and waved it in front of her.

'There's no getting anything past you, is there?' he said.

'Oh, well, that all seems to be in order. Off you go, then.'

* * *

Lizzie, who was clearly hankering after a career as a tour guide, reeled off a potted history of the university as they made their way along the avenue while Duncan, ignoring the monotonous monologue, returned his bank statement to his inside pocket.

Casting a cynical eye over the modern, white, three-storey building with floor to ceiling windows set amongst rolling, landscaped lawns, Duncan, not one to begrudge anyone anything, paused for a moment to take it all in.

'Is something the matter?' said Lizzie.

'No, no, far from it, doll. I was just thinking, you'd have landed on your feet to get a room in a place like this.'

'Aye, it's smashing, isn't it? And only a hundred pounds a week, all-in. Plus, in the main building, we've a coffee shop, a diner, a subsidised bar, live music at the weekends, and a free gym.'

'Do you not have someone to tuck you up at night, as well?'

'Sorry?'

'Nothing,' said Duncan as they reached the main door, 'I see you've got cameras up there.'

'Aye. Security here is like Big Brother.'

'Are there any inside?'

'All the way up the stairwell, and along all the corridors.'

'And who do I see about getting my hands on it?'

'Oh, I wouldn't know,' said Lizzie. 'Have a chat with Mrs McClusky, she's the lady you just met; she'll know, for sure.'

Duncan hung his head in amused disbelief as Lizzie, wary of violating the occupant's right to privacy, attempted to garner a response by delicately rapping the door with her fingernails.

'He might be sleeping,' she said, whispering as she gently turned the key in the lock. 'I'll be as quiet as I can.'

Whilst adequately furnished with a single bed, a large study desk, ample shelving, a wardrobe, and an en-suite shower room, it was clearly evident that Tarif Khan had not, anytime recently, availed himself of the laundry facilities on campus.

'He's not one for cleaning, is he?'

'Students, eh? What are we like? Okay, I'll leave you to it. If you need anything else, you know where to find me!'

Expecting Tarif Khan to appear at any moment, Duncan snapped on a pair of gloves and turned his attention to the cluttered desk where, having fingered a few well-worn text books, an iPad, and a flyer for a festival in Rozelle Park, he sat bemused by the half-empty bottle of Jack Daniels, the open bottle of Coke, and the two tumblers which, though bone dry, still reeked of whisky.

Concluding Khan to be, on the surface, no different to any other single, male, twenty-two-year-old, he eased open the drawer where, aside from some unopened mail, a roll of Sellotape, and a couple of biros, he discovered, much to his delight, a pouch of rolling tobacco and a small, silver tin containing a small lump of what he instantly recognised as cannabis resin.

Safe in the knowledge that smokers rarely wandered far from the source of their addiction, Duncan, checking his watch, settled back and awaited his return.

* * *

Surprisingly tall and seemingly malnourished, Tarif Khan, his jeans hanging from his hips, stood open-jawed in the doorway with a look of fear normally reserved for junkies who'd failed to pay their dealers whilst Duncan, nonplussed by his arrival, remained in his seat holding his warrant card aloft.

'Come in and close the door,' he said. 'I think it's time we had a wee chat, don't you?'

'What about?'

'The birds and the bees.'

Khan immediately reached for the Marlboros in his trouser pocket and fumbled for a cigarette.

'Now, now,' said Duncan, 'you'll only set the smoke alarms off, I'd wait until we're outside, if I were you. So, how's the study going?'

Unsure whether to stand or sit, Khan hovered by the door, his weight shifting nervously from one foot to the other.

'Aye. It's okay,' he said.

'And are you enjoying yourself?'

'I can't complain.'

'I know some folk who could,' said Duncan. 'I know some folk who'll look back on what was meant to be one the most exciting periods of their life and reach for the bucket.'

'They should've stayed at home.'

'You didn't. Why is that, Tarif? Why did you leave home?'

'No reason. I'm an adult. I can do what I like.'

'I'll not argue with that,' said Duncan. 'And what do you like?'

'Enjoying myself. Going out. Having a beer with my pals.'

'Beer?'

'Aye.'

'Is that why you moved out? Because your folks don't approve of your drinking?'

'Maybe.'

'And the smoking, no doubt. Are you not on the roll-ups, anymore?'

'No,' said Khan. 'I gave them up. It's too much... hassle.'

'And how's your social life? Have you got yourself a girlfriend?'

'No.'

'No? I am surprised,' said Duncan. 'A good-looking fella like yourself, I'd have thought you'd have had them swarming round you.'

'I'm not into relationships,' said Khan. 'I'm too young for that.'

'Really? I thought you were seeing a lassie called Meena?'

'Who?'

'Meena Singh-Gill.'

Khan drew hard on his unlit cigarette as his eyes darted around the room looking for somewhere to settle.

'No. I told you, I'm not ready for a relationship.'

'But she was?'

'I wouldn't know. Look, I only saw her the once. She's not my type, okay?'

'What is?'

'I'll tell you when I find out.'

'But in the meantime, you're happy to sow a few wild oats, is that it?'

Duncan leaned forward, rested his elbows on his knees, and flicked his head towards Khan's bandaged right hand.

'What happened there?' he said. 'Did you lose a bet with a chop-saw?'

Khan glanced furtively at his hand, placed it behind his back, and leaned against the wall.

'Accident,' he said. 'It's no big deal.'

'You should be more careful,' said Duncan, 'you've only got one left. You're studying journalism, is that right?'

'Sports journalism. Aye.'

'So, what's the attraction? Is it the horses? Or boxing, maybe?'

'Footy,' said Khan. 'Once I qualify, I'll get to see all the big games for free.'

'If you qualify.'

'Why wouldn't I?'

Duncan rose to his feet, pulled a pair of speedcuffs from the pouch on his belt, and stepped forward.

'Because,' he said, 'Tarif Khan, I'm arresting you under section 1 of the Criminal Justice Act on suspicion of the rape of Miss Meena Singh-Gill. You are not obliged to say anything but anything you do say will be noted and may be used in evidence. Do you understand?'

* * *

Unlike West, whose ability to burn calories like kindling in the Kalahari was almost legendary, or Munro, who could make a rib roast disappear like Penn and Teller, there came a point after a ten-hour shift where, driven by motivation alone, the only sustenance Duncan required came from a tap atop the bar in The Smoking Goat.

'Alright, pal?' he said as he ambled into the office. 'Where is everyone?'

'At this time of night?' said Dougal. 'Where do you think?'

'Alright for some. What are you up to?'

'I'm putting in for a transfer.'

'Away! Are you serious?'

'Deadly. I'm moving to the broom cupboard. Maybe that way I can get some peace.'

'Very good.'

'You might want to join me.'

'How so?'

'The Bear's been asking for you.'

'Jeez-oh!' said Duncan. 'That can only mean one thing. Is he still here?'

'In his office.'

'Right. That's me away. I need to make myself scarce.'

'Hold on!' said Dougal. 'Are you not going tell me what's going on? What happened with Khan?'

'He's downstairs,' said Duncan. 'I've not got the energy to interview him now. I'll hammer him in the morning.'

'Is he okay?'

'He's sweating,' said Duncan, 'like a wee rabbit caught in the headlights.'

'I am surprised. I had him down as a hard man.'

'You've not seen him. He's big, I'll give him that, but I've seen more meat on a butcher's apron.'

'Is it him, then?'

'Well, he'll not be playing the drums anytime soon, and if you mean, is he the fella who raped Meena Singh-Gill, then aye, I'd stake my life on it. I just need him to admit it.'

'So, what's your next move?'

'A bevvy.'

'I mean, before that.'

'Well,' said Duncan, 'I've fast-tracked his swab, and I've asked McLeod to verify he's the owner of the fingers just as soon as he gets the results.'

'Is that it?'

'Not quite,' said Duncan. 'SOCOs. They need to rip his place apart, in particular, the bed linen. He's not in the habit of changing his sheets so there's a chance we might get something off them; oh, and there's two tumblers of whisky that need testing, too.'

'You think he spiked her?'

'No, he's not the type,' said Duncan. 'Besides, Meena's all of five feet, three. It wouldn't take much to overpower her, especially after a drink or two.'

'Okay,' said Dougal. 'Well, you take yourself off and I'll sort the SOCOs for you.'

'Nice one, pal. Oh, I've also requested CCTV from the residents' block, the place is crawling with cameras. I gave them your address.'

'No bother.'

'Do you not fancy a pint? I'll stand you an orange juice.'

'No, you're alright,' said Dougal. 'I'm doing some digging on this Ross Hunter fella and it's just getting interesting.'

'Okay, if you're sure. And by the way, I'm stopping by the Singh-Gills on the way to the pub. I want to see if Meena will agree to having a sample taken from her cheek. If we do get anything from Khan's place, we're going to need something to match it to; that way we could swing a conviction even if he denies it.'

Chapter 12

Regarded by many as an impassive stalwart, a firm handshake being the closest he ever came to displaying any physical signs of affection, Munro, adept at concealing the benevolent side of his nature, preferred to show his gratitude for the help afforded him by others with discreet but meaningful acts of kindness.

He watched as a ferry silhouetted by the setting sun sliced its way across the Firth and reluctantly drained his glass as the sound of keys in the door drew him from the balcony.

'Blimey!' said West, smiling as she tossed her jacket on the sofa. 'What's been going on here?'

'I thought I'd get your house in order,' said Munro. 'There's a wash in the machine, and the rest of the laundry's in the basket in the bathroom.'

'You didn't have to do that.'

'I did, lassie. I cannae risk taking a fall at my time of life and walking around this flat is like negotiating an obstacle course. Oh, and I've made some supper, too.'

'You,' said West, 'are a bleeding Godsend! I'm blooming starving.'

'How so? Did you not get yourself a bellyful of biryani at the restaurant?'

'No, I did not. Not a sausage, tandoori or otherwise. What are we having? Please say it's not steak again.'

'No, no,' said Munro with a wily grin. 'I fetched a pie from the butcher.'

'Lovely! What kind?'

'Beef and ale.'

'I might have guessed.'

'And there's some potatoes on the boil.'

'Any veg?'

'Aye. Mashed potatoes.'

'Oh, well,' said West as she plundered the fridge, 'time to say hello to Mr John Barleycorn, then. There's nothing like an ice-cold beer to whet the appetite.'

'How did you fare with Mr and Mrs Singh-Gill?'

'Well, you'll like this. In fact, if you'd been there, you'd have probably laughed your socks off. There's no answer from the front door, right? So I whipped round the side, opened the gate, and nearly got my arm chewed off. They've got a dirty great German Shepherd in the back yard!'

'That would explain the dog food, then.'

'Yup.'

'But why a guard dog? At a restaurant?'

'They've been turned over a couple of times. Some johnnies jumping over the wall after closing and demanding all their takings.'

'And no doubt they're still waiting for uniform to investigate the matter?'

'In one,' said West as she swigged her beer. 'To be honest, I feel a bit guilty; I mean, they're a lovely couple, they probably thought I was going to ask them to cater for a party of thirty, then their jaws hit the floor when I told them they had to leave.'

'Did you give them the full story?'

'God no. They'd have been horrified. I simply said we were investigating an incident and they could have their kitchen back tomorrow – in the meantime, go home, put your feet up, and enjoy a night off. SOCOs are there now, but I'm not holding out much hope.'

'Why not?'

'Think about it,' said West, 'it's a busy kitchen. With all the cooking and cleaning they do down there, I can't see us finding any kind of DNA unless it belongs to Dolly the sheep.'

'You should know better than that, Charlie,' said Munro as he strained the spuds. 'Latent evidence can hang around for months, you'd be surprised what a humble FLS can pick up.'

'Yeah, I know,' said West, 'but I think we're going to need more than a forensic light source to crack this one. Even if we get a shedload of prints, I can guarantee they'll belong to everyone who has a legitimate right to be there. What I need is something that places Tarif Khan in that kitchen.'

'Khan?' said Munro. 'So, Duncan's struck gold, has he?'

'He sure has. I had him on the blower earlier. Khan's in custody and guess what? He's a few fingers short of a full hand.'

'That's still not enough though, is it?'

'Not by a long chalk,' said West. 'The thing is, Jimbo, even if Khan's DNA matches the fingers, all that does is prove that they're his.'

'You'll not need DNA to tell you that.'

'Either way, we still need that link between him and the Singh brothers, Ash and Navinder.'

'I think it's time you opened a bottle,' said Munro, 'it sounds like you need it.'

'Good call. Where have all the glasses gone?'

'In the cupboard, where they belong.'

West uncorked a Bordeaux, leant against the counter, and began swiping through her phone while Munro, grunting with the effort, pummelled the potatoes to a purée.

'You need to relax, Charlie,' he said. 'Put that blessed thing away for a half an hour.'

'I am relaxed! I'm just looking at some photos I took at the restaurant. They've got some lovely gear down there.'

'What do you mean, gear?'

'You know, pots and pans, and stuff. If I was into cooking, I wouldn't mind getting some myself.'

Munro cast her a sideways glance and chuckled lightly to himself.

'Dear God,' he said, 'no offence, lassie, but you? Cooking? I've more chance of witnessing the resurrection than I have seeing you make a meal from scratch.'

'Well, if I had the right tools, I might get a bit more enthusiastic about it. Look,' she said, holding the phone aloft, 'this is called a *degchi*, apparently.'

'Is it, by Christ.'

'It's used for cooking rice and stuff. And this is called a *karahi*. It's used for cooking... other stuff.'

'Riveting.'

'And look, I wouldn't mind a set of knives like these, they're kind of old-fashioned. Traditional.'

Munro glanced at the phone, dropped the masher into the pan, and pulled his spectacles from his breast pocket.

'Let me see that,' he said as he took the phone. 'Where was this?'

'Lying on the side, by the sink. Why?'

'This,' said Munro, 'is not a kitchen knife, Charlie. And it's certainly not a part of a set.'

'Well, spit it out!'

'It's a kirpan, lassie. A ceremonial dagger carried by Sikhs.'

West glared at Munro as the penny dropped.

'They didn't use a cleaver, did they?'

'If you're looking for something that places Khan inside the Punjabi Grill,' said Munro, 'then I'll wager this is it. It's probably got traces of him all over it.'

West snatched the phone and darted to the living room.

'You dish up,' she said. 'Don't wait for me, I've got a call to make.'

Happy to oblige, Munro polished off his meal, pushed his plate to one side, and sat sipping his wine while he waited for West to return.

'Sorry,' she said. 'Just had to make sure SOCOs bagged that knife. Blimey, you weren't hungry, then?'

'There's no point in serving a meal piping hot just to watch it go cold.'

'Quite right,' said West, 'but frankly, it doesn't bother me, either way.'

'I'd noticed.'

'Are you okay?'

'Aye. Why do you ask?'

'You're sweating.'

'I'm fine,' said Munro. 'Perhaps I should have let the pie cool down, after all.'

'If you say so. Right, come on then, what have you been up to behind my back?'

'I spent a very pleasant hour or two in the company of young Dougal looking at websites, in particular, the rescue centre.'

'They won't have you,' said West. 'You're too old.'

'Very good, Charlie. I see you're getting the hang of humour, at last. As it happens, I was quite taken by a cockapoo.'

'Isn't that a bird?'

'No. It's a crossbreed, to all intents and purposes, a mongrel.'

'And you're after a pure-bred, like yourself?'

'I'm not fussed,' said Munro, 'but then I happened across another wee chap. A Highland Terrier by the name of Murdo who's struggling to find a home.'

'Why? Is he vicious?'

'No, it's because he's ten, which means he's the same age as me, or thereabouts.'

'Aw, poor thing. Has he got long left?'

'Another five years, maybe.'

'And you?'

'Probably less if I hang around here much longer. No, no, I thought perhaps we could grow old together. I'm of a mind to pay him a visit tomorrow.'

'Are you serious?'

'Saving one lost soul may not change the world, Charlie, but for that one lost soul, the world will change forever.'

'Well, you've proved that already,' said West, 'but are you sure you're up to it? I mean, it's a big responsibility.'

'If I can handle a reprobate like yourself, lassie, then tending a doggie will be a walk in the park.'

'You say the nicest things. So, anything else to report apart from a morbid fascination with dying alone?'

'Aye. Peggy McClure.'

'Instead of the dog? Or as well as?'

'You're not too old for a clip round the ear; you'd be wise to remember that. She taught at the academy, up the way there.'

'That's right,' said West, topping up their glasses, 'she certainly did. She was tutoring kids with learning difficulties.'

'Well, I took a wee look at their website. Did you know they have a "where are they now?" page?'

'Sounds like the perfect place to brag about how brilliant their students are.'

'Aye, it is,' said Munro, 'and with good reason. One fellow now has a career in politics, another is something big in retail, and a young girl who launched her own brand of cosmetics is on her way to becoming a millionaire.'

'I know this is leading somewhere,' said West, 'but as usual with you, I haven't got a bleeding clue where we're going.'

'There's also a special mention for one wee lad who was accepted into boarding school.'

'And why is that such a big deal?'

'Because they took him on artistic merit alone. He was one of Peggy McClure's pupils.'

'Sorry,' said West. 'I need more than that.'

'The school in question, is Lathallan. That's where Eileen Hunter sent her son.'

'And you think it's him?'

'Could be,' said Munro. 'She said the only subject he ever excelled at was art.'

'Well, so what if it is? Sorry, Jimbo, I just don't get it, why this fuss over a coincidence?'

Munro sat back, folded his arms, and glared at West.

'Oh, here we go,' she said. 'Come on then, Bergerac, let's have it.'

'I'm saying nothing, Charlie, you figure it out.'

'You're doing my nut in, you know that?'

'What do you know about Ross Hunter?'

'A bit.'

'Then put yourself in his shoes,' said Munro. 'And I'd advise you to think carefully before you open your mouth.'

West stood, slipped her hands into her pockets, and slowly paced the room.

'Okay,' she said. 'He's a successful businessman. He's married. And he's got a son.'

'Cold.'

'Based on what you've told us, the marriage is a bit of a sham. I mean, if he's lying in his hospital bed and all Eileen Hunter can think about is missing out on her holiday, then she obviously doesn't give a toss about him.'

'Warm.'

'And then there's her son.'

'Kieran.'

'And he's not the full shilling,' said West. 'So, if she packed him off to boarding school to get him out of the way, then there's no love lost there, either.'

'Getting warmer.'

'Don't rush me,' said West, 'I'm thinking. Okay, so while Kieran's at the academy getting some special guidance from Peggy McClure, it stands to reason that Ross Hunter would've been the one to take care of things at the school, you know, liaise with the teachers, go to PTA meetings, that kind of thing.'

'Roasting.'

West turned to face Munro as the softest of smiles crept across her face.

'Ross Hunter and Peggy McClure!' she said, beaming. 'She's single, attractive, and about the same age. And he's minted and lonely! You think they were at it, don't you?'

'I'm not paid to think,' said Munro. 'You are.'

Chapter 13

One of the perks of being a night owl with borderline misanthropic tendencies – apart from the ability to focus on the job in hand unhindered by the clamorous claptrap of his affable but distracting colleagues – was an opportunity to belt out a rousing rendition of *Nessun Dorma* free from the threat of reprisals from a less than discerning audience.

With only a thin crust pepperoni, Pavarotti, and a packet of pretzels for company, Dougal, alone in the office scribbling memos on a plethora of Post-it Notes which all but obscured his screen, turned his back on his computer and awarded himself a celebratory can of Irn-Bru as the sun rose over the Clyde.

After a gruelling few hours which had him reaching for the eye drops, an intensive trawl of the records at Companies House had revealed that "R E HUNTER" of Maxwell Street, Edinburgh, had not simply relocated as purported by Mrs Eileen Hunter herself, but had in fact ceased trading before re-establishing itself as "HUNTER'S" on the west coast.

Further investigation, courtesy of his favourite tool – the images tab on his web browser – had led him to one of many blogs by amateur historians where a strikingly sharp image depicted the facade of the former premises in a state of fire-damaged disrepair, along with an unverified quote from the Fire Investigation Unit citing the cause of the blaze – despite traces of the accelerant, acetone, being found at the seat of the fire – as accidental. The blaze itself was confined to the basement stock room and the ground floor, and one casualty – a male, unidentified – was treated for second degree burns to the hands and face at The Royal Infirmary and discharged several hours later.

Keen for Mrs Hunter to attend an informal question and answer session in the sterile surroundings of the interview room, Dougal's initial joy had turned to dismay when, receiving no reply from her landline or mobile telephone, the words 'Santa Ponsa' rang alarm bells in his head.

As he'd expected, a rudimentary online search for airlines serving the island of Mallorca revealed one carrier with evening departures which were scheduled thrice weekly from Glasgow Prestwick International Airport to Palma and, despite the ungodly hour, a simple but lengthy phone call had confirmed that just one passenger, a Mr Ross Hunter, was down as a no-show, whilst another of the same name, a Mrs E Hunter, had boarded safely.

* * *

Washing down the last cold slice of congealed pizza with a drop of fizzy pop, Dougal raised the blinds and squinted at the sun as West and Munro entered the room.

'Well, if it isn't Nosferatu,' she said. 'Isn't it time you got back in your box?'

'Very funny, miss. You'll not be wanting me out of the way when you hear what I have to say.'

'Hold your horses. Here,' said West, handing him a coffee and a roll, 'you look like you could do with this. So, no sign of Duncan, yet? Dear me, the boy's slacking.'

'Anything but,' said Dougal, 'he's been with Tarif Khan for almost an hour.'

'That's a bit harsh, isn't it? Grilling the geezer at this time of the morning?'

'There's a method in his madness. He reckons he has more chance of seeing him crack if he's not had enough sleep, plus…'

'Plus what?'

'He's keeping a low profile,' said Dougal. 'The Bear's on the prowl and he's convinced he's going to get his marching orders.'

'I think I'll have a word.'

'I'd not bother if I were you, Charlie,' said Munro. 'You know Duncan, he has skin like an armadillo – nothing you can say will cheer him up.'

'I meant with Elliot. I'll see if I can get a heads-up on what's going on. After all, he might not be the only one picking up his P45. Right, come on then, sunshine, what's kept you up all night?'

Dougal glanced at the notes on his screen, took a large swig of coffee, and cleared his throat.

'I've made some headway on the Hunters,' he said. 'I've good news, and bad.'

'Well, I don't know about you, Charlie,' said Munro as he eased himself into a seat, 'but I prefer to take the bad first, anything after that can only raise your spirits.'

'Fair enough,' said West. 'Go on then, what's so grim?'

'Ross Hunter,' said Dougal. 'He passed away this morning.'

'Crap.'

'He haemorrhaged. They turned off his life support at precisely 4:19am.'

'Great. I mean, poor bugger and all that, but now we've got a murder case on our hands. That's all we need with Elliot about to show us the door.'

'Your compassion is second to none,' said Munro. 'I can see you'll not be needing tissues when they plant me in the ground.'

'Well, you know what I mean. So, have you told his missus?'

'No, no,' said Dougal, 'that's not for me to do, I'm leaving that to the hospital.'

'What about her son?'

'I've arranged for a family liaison officer to visit the school. I think it's probably best he's told face to face rather than hearing it from the headmaster. They'll be heading up there this afternoon.'

'Okay,' said West, 'so, what's the good news?'

'It's only good by comparison,' said Dougal, 'so, I'm not sure if it's going to lift your spirits that high. The Hunter's jewellery shop in Edinburgh, I think it was torched, although an unofficial report says the blaze was accidental.'

'Then what makes you think it was arson?'

'Acetone,' said Dougal. 'It's an accelerant. Traces were found at the seat of the fire but apparently it's not uncommon to have the stuff about the place. That's why they're saying it's not deliberate.'

'So, they're not here for the view after all,' said Munro. 'They moved here because they were watching their backs.'

'Possibly. Call me cynical, but if the insurance did pay out, then maybe that's how come they could afford the big, fancy house in Troon.'

'Wouldn't be the first time something like that's happened,' said West. 'Naughty buggers. There are easier ways of getting your hands on a few quid. So, I take it you've already spoken to Eileen Hunter? When's she coming in?'

'She's not coming in,' said Dougal. 'And she's not answering her phone, either.'

Munro took an aspirin from his pocket, placed it on the desk next to his coffee, and unwrapped a bacon roll.

'That's no surprise,' he said, 'as I told you before, she's probably on her way to Santa Ponsa.'

'Aye, you're on the money there, boss. She jumped the evening flight from Glasgow. I reckon she must've gone straight from the hospital to the airport.'

'Are you sure?' said West. 'What about her luggage? All her suitcases and stuff?'

'She'll not need any luggage, miss. They've a holiday home, remember? It's probably packed with everything she needs. I'm still trying to find out exactly where it is.'

'How far have you got?'

'Well, I know she picked up a Fiat 500 from Europcar in Palma, and she gave her address as the Club Nautico, so I'm getting there.'

'Of course,' said Munro, as he wired into his roll, 'there may be a quicker way of finding her. Her son, Kieran, you should give him a call.'

'What else?' said West. 'I mean, is there anything we can actually do her for apart from being a selfish cow?'

'Aye, maybe,' said Dougal, 'but I need to collate some evidence first and that may take a while.'

'Go on.'

'Ross Hunter. I think he's taken a fall before. See here, the fire at their shop in Edinburgh? There was one casualty, male, unidentified. Nothing too serious but he was treated for burns at the infirmary. I think that was him.'

'Dozy bugger,' said West. 'Probably set himself alight while he was trying to burn the place down.'

'Ordinarily, I'd agree with you,' said Dougal, 'but the thing is, the traces of acetone were on the outside of the door to the basement. He was on the inside.'

'Well, maybe the door slammed shut before he could get out.'

'Or maybe it wasnae him who set the fire at all,' said Munro. 'Dougal, you'd do well to find out exactly what kind of cover they had in place, and if Ross Hunter had any life assurance policies, too.'

'I'm already on it, boss. So, are you two hanging around or have you places to be? Folk to see?'

'If I didn't know better,' said West, 'I'd think you were trying to get rid of us.'

'No, no. Just asking, is all.'

'Well, as it happens, once we've finished our breakfast, we're going to see Peggy McClure again.'

'Again?'

'Yup. We've got a sneaky feeling that she and Ross Hunter may have been doing the dirty.'

'Jeez-oh! A crime of passion?'

'Hardly,' said Munro. 'If they were involved, then Miss McClure's not going to murder the chap she wants to be with, is she?'

'No,' said West, 'but his wife might, especially if she knew they were up to no good.'

'It's a theory, Charlie. And for the time being, that's all it is,' said Munro. 'Dougal, when you're looking into their financial affairs, dinnae stop at the insurance, you should check his personal accounts too. There's every chance he may have been giving Miss McClure a helping hand.'

Chapter 14

Without a belt to keep his jeans from falling to the floor, or any laces to keep his shoes on his feet, Tarif Khan – suffering the indignity of a dent to his ego – was singularly unique in displaying none of the bravado, arrogance, or sheer bloody-mindedness of the certified nutters, neds, and junkies it had ever been Duncan's misfortune to apprehend. Rather, he sat squirming in his seat like a twelve-year-old who'd been caught with a half a dozen Mars bars in his pocket by the owner of the local sweetshop.

'Are you okay, pal?' said Duncan. 'Do you need the toilet?'

Khan raised his head and stared at Duncan with blackened, hollow eyes.

'No,' he said, 'it's this chair. I can't get comfortable.'

'Well, it's the only one we've got, so you'll have to make do. Unless you'd prefer the floor.'

'I think I would, aye.'

Khan walked to the side of the room and, clutching the waist of his jeans with his left hand, slid down the wall and stretched out his lanky legs.

'Better?'

'Aye. Thanks.'

'Good. So, how was your bed? Did you sleep okay?'

'Not really. No.'

'Never mind,' said Duncan as he stabbed the voice recorder, 'you can get your head down later. The time is 6:05am, my name is DS Reid. For the benefit of the tape, would you state your name, please.'

'Tarif Khan.'

'Before we go any further, Tarif, you should be aware that you're entitled to legal representation. Is there anyone you'd like me to call?'

'No.'

'Would you like me to appoint a duty solicitor?'

'No.'

'Then let's crack on. Do you understand why you're here?'

'I do,' said Khan. 'You think I attacked someone.'

'Who?'

'Meena Singh-Gill.'

'But it's not simply an attack, is it?' said Duncan. 'We have reason to believe that you're guilty of rape.'

Khan looked up and wearily shook his head.

'I never raped no-one,' he said. 'Not me.'

'Okay, see here,' said Duncan, 'I'm going to let you in to a wee secret, just so's you can get your story straight. We have CCTV footage from the residential block at the uni, and forensics are examining everything in your room as we speak, so if I find out later that you've been lying to me, I'll do you for perverting the course of justice as well. Do I make myself clear?'

'I'm not lying,' said Khan, 'I've told you a hundred times, I never laid a finger on her.'

Duncan leaned back in his seat, folded his arms, and regarded Khan with a look of condemnation.

'That's not what Meena says,' he said, like a judge resigned to passing a guilty verdict. 'She wants to press…'

'That's tosh!' said Khan. 'You're winding me up!'

'I wish I was, but as I was saying, she's about to press formal charges against you. However, if you come clean now, then maybe…'

'Get it up you!' said Khan. 'Why? Tell me, why would she do that?'

'I'd have thought that was pretty obvious.'

'I would never harm Meena, we're pals, and we have been ever since school.'

'Well, maybe you took your friendship a bit too far. Maybe you overstepped the mark.'

'You've not listened to a single word I've said, have you? For the hundredth time, I'm not into her.'

'I thought she had the hots for you?'

'As a friend, aye.'

'Are you saying you don't believe she was raped?'

'I'm saying nothing of the sort,' said Khan. 'Meena's as straight as a die. If she says she was raped, then she was. It just wasn't me.'

'That's right, I remember now,' said Duncan. 'She's not your type.'

Khan rubbed the back of his head, took a deep breath, and hesitated before speaking.

'She's not my gender.'

Duncan, feeling as though he'd just stuck his tongue on the positive terminal of a twelve-volt battery, sat up straight and leaned across the table.

'Are you saying what I think you're saying?'

'Oh, here we go,' said Khan. 'Don't tell me you're homophobic.'

'I'm homo nothing, pal. Whatever floats your boat, it's nothing to do with me.'

'I'm glad to hear it.'

'So, when I asked you earlier if you had a girlfriend, and you said no, you were being honest with me?'

'Aye, of course,' said Khan. 'Why would I lie?'

'Then let me rephrase the question, Tarif. Do you have a boyfriend?'

'Sort of. I'm in a relationship. A very casual relationship.'

'So, it's not serious?'

'It's fun.'

'And would you mind telling me his name?'

'Why?'

'No reason. There's no obligation. But a good character reference can always come in handy.'

Khan glanced furtively at Duncan and paused before answering.

'His name's Ash.'

'Ash? You mean Ashar Singh-Gill? Meena's brother?'

Khan's shoulders began to tremble like somebody on the verge of a nervous breakdown as he tried to suppress his laughter.

'She's not his sister!' he said, giggling. 'They're not even related!'

'Whoa! Whoa! Whoa! Back up, pal! What do you mean, they're not even related?'

Khan spun on the floor to face Duncan and pulled his knees to his chest.

'Mr Singh-Gill was widowed when Ash and Nav were weans, okay? He met Anisha, that's Mrs Singh-Gill, a few years ago. They fell in love and got married.'

'I'm not with you,' said Duncan. 'How does…'

'Anisha's a divorcee! Meena's her daughter from the previous marriage!'

'So, she's their stepsister?'

'At last. He gets it.'

'Well, that's a revelation,' said Duncan. 'A revelation indeed. So, do they get along? As a family?'

'They used to.'

'Used to? So, what happened?'

Khan turned his back to the wall, lowered his legs, and shrugged his shoulders.

'Listen,' said Duncan, 'now's not the time to clam up, okay? Something you said or did was bad enough to make

Ash and Navinder come after you and I need to know what it was.'

'Ash had nothing to do with it.'

'So, it was Nav?'

'I'm saying nothing.'

'Are you for real?' said Duncan. 'Some fella slices your fingers off, maims you for life, and you're not saying anything? How so?'

'Because,' said Khan, 'I'm not into retribution.'

'Not you, maybe, but the other fella obviously is.'

Frustrated by Khan's sudden reluctance to co-operate further, Duncan stepped from behind the desk and squatted by the opposite wall.

'I'm struggling here,' he said as he ruffled his hair, 'there's something you're not telling me and it's making things harder for the both of us so, unless you want to go back to your cell for another twelve hours, I'm just going to sit here until you're ready to talk. It's no skin off my nose, I've got all day.'

Khan toyed with the bandage on his left hand, glanced furtively at Duncan, and nodded towards the desk.

'Can we turn that off?' he said.

Duncan shook his head and smiled.

'No need,' he said. 'Listen, pal, even if you do decide to tell me who chopped your hand off, we can't do anything about it unless you yourself want to file charges, do you understand? And as for Meena, between you and me, I really don't think you did it, so you've nothing to worry about, okay?'

Torn between a fear of reprisals, protecting his friends, and justice being served on the perpetrator for what was nothing less than a heinous crime, Khan took a deep breath and dived in.

'It was about a month ago,' he said. 'A Friday night. I was at their house. Their folks were at the restaurant, as usual, so we had the place to ourselves. It was pure quality, just the four of us, plenty of booze, and some cracking tunes.'

'Okay. Go on.'

'It was just the back of nine. Meena wanted to call it a night. She was that hammered, she could hardly stand.'

'So she went to bed and the three of you carried on?'

'For a bit,' said Khan, 'then about a half an hour later a couple of lads turned up.'

'Gatecrashers?'

'No, no. They were invited, apparently. Navinder's pals. They looked like they'd just come from work.'

'How so?'

'Scruffy. Dressed like builders.'

'So, I take it Nav doesn't move in the same circles as yourself?'

'Certainly not,' said Khan, 'he likes to think of himself as an alpha-male; you know the type, all football chants and chat-up lines.'

'So, these two lads, did you know them?'

'No.'

'How about Ash?'

'I'm not sure,' said Khan, 'but he definitely recognised them. He said they were trouble and we should leave.'

'Why?'

'Put it this way, the first thing they said when they came in the room, was "alright girls".'

'A couple of dunderheids, then?'

'Aye, exactly. So, me and Ash took ourselves off to the pub, had a couple of bevvies, then he came back with me and crashed at mine.'

'So you left Navinder to it?' said Duncan. 'With his pals?'

'Aye.'

'And then?'

'And then what? That's it. Until I saw Meena at college.'

'And that was on the Monday?'

'Aye. But she wasn't herself,' said Khan, 'I could tell. We skipped a lecture and went to my room for a wee chat, and that's when she told me what had happened.'

'And what did happen?'

'I told you. I'm not saying.'

'Okay,' said Duncan, 'then I'm guessing whatever it was that Meena told you, sometime sooner or later, you told Ash. Am I right?'

'Aye. But not straight away, I mean, she told me in confidence. I was going off my head trying to decide what I should do, then eventually I thought it was probably best if I told him.'

'And when was that?'

'A couple of weeks later.'

'And what did Ash do? Did he confront Navinder?'

'Maybe.'

'So, that's why he came after you,' said Duncan, 'to shut you up. See here, Tarif, this is all making perfect sense now, but what I don't get is how you can sit there and not give a damn about Meena's attacker, I mean, are you okay with that? Really?'

'It's not my call!' said Khan, his voice wavering. 'It's Meena's choice, and I have to respect that!'

'Aye, well, that's all very noble of you,' said Duncan, 'but in the meantime there's a rapist out there wandering the streets. Tell me something, Tarif, do you have a sister?'

'Oh, that's not fair!'

'Life's not fair, pal, but that's the way you have to look at it. How would you feel if something happened to her?'

'I'd be raging, sure!'

'Then maybe you should start thinking about her,' said Duncan, 'you'd be doing her a favour. Now, why did you meet Nav at the Punjabi Grill? Why not somewhere safe? Somewhere neutral?'

'It was his idea.'

'So, at this point you had no idea why he wanted to meet?'

'None,' said Khan. 'It never even crossed my mind that it was to do with Meena. All I knew was that he'd been to our shops looking for me, saying it was urgent. I thought maybe he wanted me to cover his shift or something?'

'And you've done that before?'

'Not for Nav, no. But I've helped Ash out a few times.'

'Okay, so what happened when you got there?'

'I wandered through the kitchen,' said Khan, 'he laughed and smiled like nothing was wrong and tossed me an aubergine. He told me to slice it up and start salting it.'

'Then what?'

'Then it's all a bit of a blur. Next thing I know he's beside me, he's got my hand flat against the chopping board, and that was it. They were gone.'

'Did you not scream the place down?' said Duncan. 'By Christ, surely that must've hurt?'

'The funny thing is, no. It didn't hurt, not that much. There was just this kind of... throbbing.'

'Were you not scared?'

'Are you joking me?' said Khan. 'I was cacking myself. That's when I figured it had something to do with Meena. I thought he was going to slit my throat.'

'Did he threaten you?'

'Oh, aye. Big time. He said that if I said anything to anyone, I'd have to get myself a guide dog. And then a wheelchair.'

Assuming Navinder Singh-Gill to be a closet psychopath, and Tarif Khan to be either incredibly brave or astoundingly stupid, Duncan returned to his seat and stared pensively into space.

'Well, I've got to hand it you,' he said as he pawed the stubble on his chin, 'you've got some balls, I'll give you that, but tell me this, why did he only hack off three fingers?'

'Three?' said Khan. 'No, no. They all went. All four.'

'We only found three.'

'Then maybe that mangy dog they keep in the yard got something extra with his supper.'

'Have you seen a doctor?' said Duncan, allowing himself a wry smile. 'If you're not careful, that could turn nasty.'

Khan nodded.

'My uncle.'

'Your uncle? Is he a qualified first-aider?'

'Better than that, he's a GP.'

'A GP? That's a wee bit convenient, is it not?'

'We've got all the bases covered, Sergeant,' said Khan. 'Within our family we've got a doctor, an accountant, a solicitor, a dentist, and an estate agent. His surgery's on Allison Street. I legged it round there straight afterwards.'

'Was he not curious about your injury?'

'He's family,' said Khan. 'Old school. Ask no questions, know what I mean?'

'Aye, fair enough. But even so, I mean, you must have been screaming your head off.'

'Like I said, it wasn't that bad. I was probably in too much shock.'

'But he took care of you?'

'He did, aye,' said Khan. 'He stitched me up, gave me some painkillers, and a week's worth of antibiotics. With a bit of luck, I should be okay.'

'You're a lucky man,' said Duncan, 'I'm not sure they'd have kept quiet about it down at the hospital. Okay, one more thing before you go. If Ash had nothing to do with this, then why was he riding a stolen moped?'

'Because Nav's a numpty,' said Khan. 'He can't even ride a bicycle. Ash was just the driver. Trust me, he didn't have a scooby what Nav was up to.'

'Okay, but why a moped? I mean, why steal a moped? They're not short of cash, there's other ways they could've got around town.'

'And just casually walk in and out of the shops?' said Khan. 'Don't be daft. Nav had to be in and out as quick as he could without being recognised.'

'Sorry,' said Duncan, 'but something's not quite adding up here. If Navinder was that keen to get a hold of you, why did he not just ask Ash to give you a bell?'

'Are you mad? That would've been like admitting he was guilty. Besides, Ash would've got suspicious.'

'Oh, right, you mean he didn't get suspicious when Nav asked him for a lift to all your family's shops?'

'No,' said Khan. 'Why would he? He doesn't know what my family do, and even if he did, he'd not find them in the shops.'

'How so?'

'My folks sit on their backsides all day long watching the telly, they get their relations to run the shops. Aunts, uncles, brothers, sisters, first cousins, second cousins.'

'That's plenty,' said Duncan. 'I get the picture.'

Khan hauled himself to his feet and stood holding his jeans by the waist.

'Is that us?' he said. 'Only, I could use the bathroom.'

'Aye, that's us,' said Duncan, 'but see here, Tarif, if I'm keeping your name out of this, then I need a favour in return.'

'What kind of favour?'

'You're not to wander far from your digs, have you got that? I may need to speak to you again.'

'No bother.'

'And second, you're to stay away from Navinder, okay?'

'Aye, no danger there. Trust me.'

'Good. Okay, let's get you fed and watered, then you're free to go.'

Chapter 15

Content to spend his evenings as an errant teen languishing in the park with a bottle of Buckfast rather than reading, revising, or helping with the housework, Duncan – lest he fall victim to a skelping from his parents – had soon perfected the art of sneaking back to his bedroom with the stealth of a feral cat; a skill which had subsequently proved invaluable since graduating as a fully-fledged officer of the law.

Brimming with apprehension, he eased open the door, peered inside, and slipped silently into his seat, causing Dougal to jump as his chair scraped across the floor.

'Jeez-oh!' he said. 'Are you trying to kill me?'

'Sorry, pal, I had to make sure the coast was clear.'

'How so?'

'The Bear.'

'Oh, you're alright,' said Dougal, 'I've not seen him. Are you okay? You look done in.'

'Aye, I'm pure shattered, that's all. This business with Tarif Khan – it's not a can of fingers we're dealing with anymore, it's a can of worms.'

'Do you want to run through it?'

'Aye, but not just now,' said Duncan, 'there's somewhere I have to be. How are you getting on?'

'Like yourself, my head's mince, but I did get to speak with Hunter's wean, Kieran.'

'It must be hard for the lad. How's he bearing up?'

'Well, he sounded surprisingly well,' said Dougal. 'I'm thinking that maybe, because he's not seen his folks in a while, it's not hit him as hard as I thought it might.'

'Aye, right enough,' said Duncan. 'Distance. It doesn't make the heart grow fonder. Just colder.'

'I never knew you were such a romantic.'

'So, is he heading home to Troon?'

'No, no. He has no-one to mind him so he's stopping at the school for now, but he did give me the details of their place in Santa Ponsa. It's a three-bed duplex right on the harbour. He even gave me the number of the concierge.'

'Oh, I'd not call him,' said Duncan. 'She'll get the fear if she thinks someone's after her. Have you not tried her mobile again?'

'No point. If she wasn't picking up yesterday, then why should she answer now?'

'Because, you dafty, yesterday she was 30,000 feet in the air, and if she's anything like the chief said she was, then she'd have headed straight for the bar and spent the evening knocking back Cuba Libres.'

'Oh, I never thought of it like that,' said Dougal.

'You need some rest, pal, you're not thinking straight. Listen, before you call her, I need a wee favour. Can you arrange for that Navinder Singh-Gill to get picked up?'

'No bother.'

'I've still not spoken to him and after what Khan's just told me, it's what you might call urgent. Oh, and where's Westy? I need to bring her up to speed with what's happened.'

'The recycling centre,' said Dougal. 'She's away to see Peggy McClure.'

'Is she with the chief?'

'No, he's on a mission of mercy.'

'Sorry?'

'The rescue centre. He's after getting himself a wee doggy.'

'Which one?'

'A Scottish Terrier.'

'No, you numpty. Which centre?'

'Oh, it's in the middle of nowhere, somewhere near Cumnock, I think. Will I text you the address?'

'Aye, go on, and if Westy calls, tell her to stay put. I'm on the way.'

* * *

Standing with her legs akimbo and her waterproof coveralls rolled down to the waist, Peggy McClure, brandishing a high-powered pressure washer like a guerrilla unloading a Kalashnikov, grinned maniacally as the jet hammered the inside of an upturned wheelie bin causing West to shield her ears from the deafening din.

'Spillage!' said McClure, yelling as she turned it off. 'Lord knows what it was but I'm not taking any chances. There's no telling what some folk use their empty bottles for.'

'Tell me about it,' said West. 'When I was at college there was this bloke who couldn't be bothered using the bathroom at night so he...'

'That's plenty!' said McClure. 'Have you not got your pal with you? That Mr Munro?'

'Afraid not, he's busy.'

'Pity. I thought he might be up for a spot of dog walking.'

'Oh, he is, but I think he's taking care of that himself.'

'Sorry, you've lost me.'

'Doesn't matter,' said West. 'Listen, can you spare a couple of minutes?'

'Aye, no bother,' said McClure, nodding towards the bench. 'Let's have a seat and enjoy the sunshine while we can. So, how can I help?'

'It's going back a bit, I know, so if you can't remember, then no sweat, but it's about your time at the academy. One of your pupils, to be precise.'

'Oh, aye. Who's that then?'

'A kid by the name of Kieran Hunter.'

'Kieran!' said McClure, breaking into a smile. 'I remember him like it was yesterday.'

'Oh?'

'Gifted is the word I'd use. I'm telling you, that boy had talent beyond his years.'

'Really?'

'He'd give Monet a run for his money.'

'I see,' said West, 'but then, why did he need your help?'

'Because he couldn't keep up,' said McClure, 'in class, I mean. He had trouble communicating. It's called ASD.'

'ASD? What's that? Some kind of autism?'

'Aye! Well done, that's exactly what it is. Kieran wasn't stupid, not by any stretch of the imagination, he just preferred to live in his own world rather than ours.'

'Is that why he was so interested in painting?'

'One of the reasons, aye.'

'It's a good job he had someone like you to look after him, then,' said West. 'Someone who understood.'

'Well, I did my best although, truth be told, some folk didn't appreciate my efforts.'

'Oh? Like who?'

McClure glanced at West and shook her head.

'His mother,' she said. 'She thought she'd given birth to Einstein but when poor Kieran couldn't achieve his grades, she gave up. I hate to say it but she basically treated him like an unwanted pet.'

'What? Even though she knew about his condition?'

105

'Oh, aye. She didn't care a hoot. I'm telling you, if he'd been born with a receipt, she'd have taken him back for a refund.'

'Charming,' said West. 'And what about his dad? Was he the same?'

'Good grief, no! Chalk and cheese,' said McClure. 'No-one could've loved that lad more than he.'

'So you remember him, too?'

'How could I forget? It made my day, seeing the way he doted on that boy.'

'What can you tell me about him?'

'Ross? Where shall I begin?' said McClure. 'Kind, caring, generous, a wicked sense of humour, and between you and me, quite a looker, too.'

'Sounds like quite a catch,' said West. 'Mrs Hunter must've been made up to have married him.'

'Aye, you'd have thought so, but no, I'm not convinced about that.'

'How come?'

'You can tell; you know what it's like. The way they carried on, their body language. They only ever came to the school as a couple twice, and it was clear to me that their marriage was not a match made in heaven. As far as I could see, he couldn't do or say anything right.'

'Blimey,' said West, 'that must have been a bit embarrassing; for you, I mean.'

'Aye, you're not wrong there,' said McClure. 'So, is that why you're here? Are they divorced or something?'

West shifted in her seat and scratched the top her head.

'Not quite,' she said. 'I've got a bit of bad news, I'm afraid. Ross Hunter, he's passed away.'

McClure froze and stared at West as the news sank in.

'Oh dear,' she said as her shoulders slumped. 'Oh, dear, dear, dear. That's terrible, that. What happened? Was it an accident?'

'Of sorts. Obviously I can't say much at the moment. You understand.'

'Aye, of course. So, you think there was something fishy about his death, is that it?'

'Like I said.'

'Sorry.'

West turned to face McClure, stretched an arm along the back of the bench, and lowered her voice.

'Look,' she said, 'don't take this the wrong way, but did you and Mr Hunter… how can I put it? Did the two of you ever… socialise?'

'You mean go for a wee bevvy? That kind of thing?'

'Yeah, exactly.'

'We did, aye.'

'Often?'

'As often as we could,' said McClure. 'We had regular meetings, a couple of times a month after school to discuss Kieran's progress. Ross was always on his own so we'd nip along to the pub instead of sitting in the classroom. It made it seem less formal.'

'Okay, and did you ever do anything more than hit the pub, like, I don't know, go out for dinner, maybe?'

McClure sat back, folded her arms, and regarded West with a wry smile.

'Is that not a wee bit personal?'

'Yup, it certainly is,' said West, 'but it's informal too. Strictly off the record. You don't have to answer, if you don't want to.'

'But why? Why are you interested in what me and Ross got up to? Am I under some kind of suspicion for something?'

'Don't be daft,' said West, 'nothing of the sort. I'm just trying to get an idea of what he was like, you know, interests, temperament, that kind of thing.'

'Oh well,' said McClure, 'if that's all you're after, then no…'

McClure's words tailed off as her colleague, avoiding the puddles on the ground, zig-zagged his way towards them bearing two mugs of tea.

'Elevenses,' he said. 'Sorry, if I'd known you had company, I'd have brought another.'

'You've not met, have you?' said McClure. 'Inspector, this is Gordon Miller. Gordy, Inspector West.'

'Alright, hen? Here, you can have mine if you like, it's milk and two.'

'I'm alright, thanks,' said West. 'So, you're the bloke who helped Peggy find the fingers?'

'Aye, that's me,' said Miller. 'Not the best experience I've ever had, I can tell you.'

'No, I'm sure it wasn't. I understand you check over all the CCTV footage as well?'

'I do indeed. As my technological skills know no bounds, it falls to me to do the detective work.'

'And are you good at it?'

'One hundred per cent,' said Miller. 'I'm like a Mountie, me, I always get my man. Or woman.'

'That's Gordy for you,' said McClure. 'Modest to a T.'

'And how about you, Inspector?' said Miller. 'Are you any good? Did you find out who they belonged to?'

'We certainly did,' said West. 'Peggy's just filling me in on a few details.'

'That's right,' said McClure, 'I've told her everything she needs to know.'

'Not everything, I hope,' said Miller with a wink. 'Right, I'll leave you to it. I'll be round back if you need me.'

'Sorry about that, Gordy's what you might call the inquisitive type. So, where were we?'

'You and Ross. Dinner?'

'Oh aye, dinner. We did go out, a few times, nothing fancy mind, just a pub meal or a pizza.'

'And was this to discuss Kieran, too?'

'No, no. It was purely pleasure. I used to enjoy myself, he was good company.'

'And once Kieran had gone to Lathallan, what happened then? Did you continue to see each other?'

'We did,' said McClure. 'In fact, it was Ross who suggested it, he couldn't wait. I think deep down he was a wee bit depressed and lonely, you know?'

'All too well,' said West, muttering under her breath. 'Okay, Peggy, here's the nub. Tell me to mind my own business if you like but did you and Ross... did you ever get close?'

Peggy laughed out loud and looked towards the sky as if reminiscing about a childhood sweetheart.

'You're asking, did we ever sleep together? Well, I'm sorry to say the answer to that question is a resounding no. We never even kissed, and more's the pity.'

'So, you were quite fond of him then?'

'Oh aye,' said McClure, 'I'll not deny it. But that's the kind of fella he was. Decent. He said as long as he was married, he'd not get involved with anyone.'

'You make it sound as though you drifted apart.'

'We did. With Kieran away, he spent all his spare time travelling up to see him, and when he was here, he was trying to keep his wife happy, so the calls got fewer and fewer, and in the end, that was that.'

'So, when was the last time you saw him?'

'Oh, I've not seen him for months, a year maybe.'

'He was a jeweller, right?'

'Aye, he was,' said McClure. 'Not in the strict sense of the word, I mean, he didn't make the stuff himself, but he had a wee shop.'

'And just out of interest, did he ever buy you anything? You know, surprise you with a present, maybe?'

'The only thing Ross Hunter ever bought me,' said McClure with a grin, 'was a large gin and tonic. Oh, and this.'

McClure raised her left hand so West could inspect the single, square-cut diamond set on a platinum band.

'Blimey,' said West, 'that's a bit tasty. Must've cost a few quid.'

'I wouldn't know,' said McClure. 'He said it was the least he could do – for taking care of Kieran.'

'Well, I've heard of tipping the staff, but that takes the biscuit. Tell me, though, if you're still single, why do you wear it on that finger?'

'It keeps the neds away,' said McClure. 'They'll not come near me if they think I've a fella indoors.'

Chapter 16

With his hands clasped firmly behind his back and his face tilted up towards the sun, Munro, surrounded by acre upon acre of rolling, green farmland, smiled contentedly as he strolled across the field like a laird on a constitutional whilst his prospective partner – stopping, turning, and waiting without the need for a leash or a whistle – ambled obediently by his side.

Pausing for a breather, he squatted on his haunches and offered the hound a small piece of broccoli followed by a green bean and a slice of carrot, all of which were flatly refused in favour of a beef-flavoured treat.

'I see you and I are cut from the same cloth,' he said as the terrier raised a paw. 'Kindred spirits, you might say. Aye, that's the word, kindred.'

Distracted by a dishevelled figure waving from beyond the hedgerow, Munro stood and, recognising the bedraggled scruff as one of his own, beckoned him over, his raised palm advising him to proceed with caution.

'Well, hello wee man!' said Duncan as the dog leapt to greet him. 'And who the devil are you?'

'This,' said Munro, 'is Murdo. Murdo, this sartorially-challenged gentleman is Detective Sergeant Reid. You'll be seeing a lot of each other, no doubt.'

'He's a cracker, chief! Are you taking him?'

'Oh, I cannae refuse him now. We have what I believe folk in these circles call a bond.'

'I'm made up for you. Have you sorted all the paperwork?'

'Not yet, but there's no rush. They said we could walk out here for as long as we like.'

'Well, it's too good a day to be stuck indoors,' said Duncan, 'just mind he doesn't overheat.'

'How so?'

'Heatstroke, chief. Dogs are susceptible to it, especially the older ones. See here, it might seem like a pleasant day to you and me but they suffer in the heat. If you do take him out in this kind of weather, be sure to walk him in the shade, and make sure you've always got a bottle of water with you.'

'Well, I'm indebted to you, laddie,' said Munro. 'I never realised.'

'Oh, I'm sure they would've told you before you left. Will we walk a while?'

'Aye, we should,' said Munro. 'You've obviously got something on your mind.'

'How can you tell?'

'Why else would you be traipsing across a field in the middle of nowhere with a retired copper and a pensionable dog?'

'Fair do's,' said Duncan. 'I need to tap your brain; some advice is what I'm after.'

'I'll do my best. So, what's the story?'

'Meena Singh-Gill,' said Duncan. 'I'll not bore you with the details just now but I interviewed Tarif Khan earlier and if he's telling the truth, which I believe he is, then we've another likely scenario on our hands which is complicating things.'

112

'Go on.'

'Okay. Until this morning we knew that her stepbrother, Navinder…'

'Hold on,' said Munro. 'Stepbrother?'

'Aye. It turns out they're not related after all. Anyway, we've always assumed that he was alone with her in the house the night that she was attacked.'

'But?'

'But she wasn't,' said Duncan. 'According to Khan, two of Nav's pals turned up. Now, I've not spoken to Navinder yet so we've no idea who these fellas are, but it is possible that one, two, or all three of them may have been involved in the assault.'

'By jiminy!' said Munro, his lip curling in disgust. 'That's exactly the kind of thing that makes my blood boil! Dear God, if I had my way, I'd castrate the lot of them! So, what's the problem?'

'Evidence, chief. Or rather, a lack of it.'

'And Meena Singh-Gill, I take it she's been to the clinic?'

'She has indeed. Fair play to the lass, she didn't say she'd been attacked, just that she didn't feel right. They examined her and said she should have a wee word with her husband or her partner, and tell them not to be so rough in the future.'

'And of course, she doesnae have a husband or a partner.'

'Precisely,' said Duncan. 'So, although it proves that something definitely happened, if she'll not let an FME go near her, how do we go about gathering any evidence?'

Munro, short of advising Duncan to intimidate Navinder Singh-Gill in an effort to extract a confession, proffered instead the only legal means he had of identifying the perpetrator.

'At the risk of stating of the obvious, laddie,' he said, continuing on his way, 'I'd say your best bet, for the time being at least, is the bed linen and whatever Miss Singh-Gill was wearing at the time.'

'I've already thought of that,' said Duncan, 'and frankly, it's not worth the effort.'

'Why not?'

'Oh chief, it was almost a month ago! She'd have washed them by now, if she's not burned them!'

Munro took a tennis ball from his pocket, tossed it across the field, and smiled as Murdo ran to fetch it.

'Tell me,' he said, casting Duncan a sideways glance, 'what's the most valuable tool you have at your disposal? As a police officer, I mean. Aside from your instinct?'

'Tough call,' said Duncan, 'but if I had to choose, then I'd have to say my money's on a Taser.'

'Experience, you balloon! And as you've just proved, it's something you're sorely lacking, so I shall give you the benefit of mine.'

'On you go, I'm all ears.'

'Body fluids,' said Munro. 'Blood, saliva, semen, even DNA, they can all be retrieved from garments after they've been laundered.'

'Are you joking me?'

'I kid you not. Now, dinnae raise your hopes, laddie, the hotter the wash, and the longer it's been, the harder it is.'

'But it's still possible?'

'More than possible,' said Munro. 'There's been plenty of cases where they've picked up DNA from garments that have been through the wash eight or even nine months after the event.'

'Magic!' said Duncan. 'Chief, I owe you, big time!'

'Well, you can pay me back now, laddie. Do you have your telephone with you?'

'Aye, of course. Shall I dial the number for you?'

'It's not a call I'm after, it's a pet shop. The nearest one to here.'

'No bother, hold on and I'll look. What are you needing?'

'Dog food, best of gear mind, not that cheap rubbish.'

'Will the folk here not give you some?'

'Aye, a wee bit,' said Munro, 'but only enough for a few days.'

'Is that it?'

'No, no. I shall be needing a new lead, too. And a collar. And a dog tag. And a bed. And a coat. A brush, a comb, oh, and a few squeaky things to keep him occupied.'

'Jeez-oh,' said Duncan, 'it's worse than shopping for a bairn.'

'I've not had the pleasure,' said Munro, 'which is why this wee fellow is about to be spoilt rotten.'

* * *

Mopping her brow and wishing she'd dressed for a week in Waikiki, West, looking like a roadie in her black jeans and tee shirt, sat sweltering in the Defender as she waited for Duncan to arrive, groaning as her body clock chimed lunch o'clock.

'At last,' she said, jumping from the car as the Audi pulled up behind her. 'Couldn't this have waited until we got back to the office? I'm flipping starving!'

'Not really, miss,' said Duncan, 'I'm on a flyer.'

'Really? Because from where I'm standing it looks as though you're trying to avoid the place.'

'Aye, well, there is that too, I suppose.'

'Well, relax,' said West. 'I'm going to have a word with Elliot later so I can get an update and put us all out of our misery. So, what's up? Why are you in such a hurry?'

'I had a chat with Tarif Khan this morning; the bottom line is, he's in the clear…'

'You're sure?'

'Positive, but he says there were two other fellas at Meena's place when the assault took place, pals of

Navinder's, so they may have been involved in the attack too.'

'Too?' said West. 'What do you mean, *too*?'

'I mean, Navinder may not have acted alone.'

'Alright, slow down, speedy. You're not seriously suggesting that she was raped by her own brother?'

'Stepbrother, miss. They're not related.'

'Blimey,' said West, 'this is turning into the bleeding Jeremy Kyle show.'

'Right enough, that's why I went for a word with the chief.'

'Jimbo? What for?'

'Advice.'

'Charming. You could have come to me, you know.'

'Aye, but with all due respect, you were busy.'

'Well, try me now.'

'Okay,' said Duncan. 'DNA retrieval from laundered garments, is it possible?'

'Is it possible?' said West with a half-hearted laugh. 'What kind of a question is that? Alright, you've got me. Is it?'

'Aye, it is,' said Duncan, 'and the good news is, I just got off the phone with Meena, I'm away to collect her belongings now.'

'I'm surprised she's still got them.'

'You and me both.'

'So, where is this Navinder geezer now?'

'Dougal called him in, he's in the custody suite. I'll interview him when I get back.'

'I think I might join you,' said West. 'And Meena? What's the score with her?'

'She'll still not see a forensic medical examiner, but she has been to the clinic.'

'And the upshot is?'

'She was definitely, how can I put this, interfered with.'

'So, do we know who Navinder's mates are?'

'I'm hoping to find out within the hour.'

'Alright,' said West, 'you get a wiggle on, and I'll see you back at the office.'

'Roger that, and oh, if you're stopping for lunch, I could go for a burger and fries myself. I'll settle with you later.'

Chapter 17

Cursing Munro for saying she'd need no more than a sou'wester and a decent pair of wellington boots if she were to join him north of the border, a tetchy West – suffering from the combined effects of heat and hunger – had soon learned that, contrary to popular belief, Scotland, whilst famed for its showers, enjoyed more than its fair share of blistering sunshine as well.

Almost suffocating from the lack of air, she stormed across the office and opened all the windows in a bid to alleviate the stifling atmosphere.

'It's like bleeding Kew Gardens in here!' she said, scowling at Dougal as she dumped a brown, paper sack on her desk. 'Aren't you hot?'

'No, not really,' he said. 'You see, miss, the trick is not to move around too much.'

'Well, you've got that off to a fine art,' said West as she unpacked the bag. 'Right, I've got two quarter pounders, two double cheeseburgers, two chicken wraps, some fries, Coke, and an Irn-Bru.'

'Did you not get anything for us?'

'A right hook, if you're not careful. You'd better dive in before Duncan gets back, his appetite's worse than mine. Any sign of Jimbo?'

'The dog whisperer? No, not yet.'

'Well, I hope he gets approved or he'll be as miserable as sin.'

'Misery I can deal with,' said Dougal, 'but I'm not sure about a dog.'

'Why not? Are you allergic?'

'No, I'm just more of a cat man, myself.'

'That figures,' said West, 'they like skulking about in the dark too. So, how are you getting on?'

'On a scale of one to ten? Nine point nine.'

'Room for improvement, then.'

'I'll start with the car at the jewellers.'

'A white hatchback, wasn't it?'

'That's right,' said Dougal, 'and if you remember, the witness said it had a black cross on the front.'

'Yeah, so what was that?' said West. 'Graffiti? Some kind of religious icon?'

'Very good, but no. At least I don't think so. I've looked at every single make and model of hatchback on the market and I'm convinced the motor they're talking about is a Toyota. To be precise, an Aygo. The black cross is a feature of the bodywork below the bonnet.'

'Well done, you. Okay, let's say for the sake of argument that you're right, where does that leave us?'

'Well,' said Dougal, 'if we assume that the perp hasn't travelled all the way from Timbuktu but lives locally, by which I mean Ayrshire, then only four white versions with a black trim were registered here last year. I've cross-checked the keepers' details from the DVLA with the electoral register, so we're good to go.'

'Go where?'

'Door to door, miss. It's the only way we'll find out if any of the owners match the fella on the footage from the security cameras.'

'Well, we needn't waste our time doing that,' said West, 'we'll get uniform to sort it for us, it shouldn't take long.'

'Aye, right enough,' said Dougal, 'but there's something you should know. It's not looking promising, even I say so myself.'

'Why not?'

'Of the four owners, there's only one single fella amongst them, another's married, and then there's a couple of pensioners, and a single female.'

'Oh, use your noddle,' said West, 'it makes no difference if they're married or not! The perp could've borrowed it, or he might be someone's son or boyfriend! Let's move on, what's happening with Eileen Hunter?'

'She's still not answering her phone, but I did speak to her son and he's given me details of their apartment in Santa Ponsa.'

'And how is he? Kieran?'

'Aye, okay. Quite chirpy, in fact. Very polite, he was even asking after his old teacher.'

'McClure?'

'Aye.'

'She must have had some influence on him, but then again, we all remember our favourite teachers, don't we? Mine was a bloke called Bonnington, he taught biology and he had these big, brown eyes. All he had to do was look at me and I'd...'

'That's plenty.'

'Sorry, I'm getting carried away. Anyway, Eileen Hunter?'

'I've my doubts about the pair of them,' said Dougal. 'Her and her husband.'

'Explain.'

'Their shop in Edinburgh? The insurance paid out, after all. Plenty, as it happens.'

'How much?'

'Just shy of a half a million.'

'Half a million! Blimey, no wonder she's swanning around like lady muck.'

'That's what happens when your valuable stock goes up in flames – if indeed it did.'

'So that's how come they could afford that fancy pile in Troon.'

'Aye, I'd agree with you there,' said Dougal, 'but we need something concrete on her, something to do with Ross Hunter, if we're to request a European Arrest Warrant to bring her back.'

West took a sip of Coke, tossed the wrapper from a quarter pounder into the wastepaper basket, and picked up a cheeseburger.

'The question is,' she said, wiping a dollop of ketchup from the side of her mouth, 'why? Why would someone hammer Ross Hunter over the head, and more importantly, walk away as if nothing had happened?'

'Maybe it was a hit,' said Dougal. 'Maybe somebody was paid to do it.'

'Then why didn't they finish him off? Why didn't they make sure he was dead before they left? You're sure there's no nutters on the loose? No-one on day release who hasn't gone home?'

'No, no-one,' said Dougal. 'But one thing I am certain of is that it has to do with money; there's no other reason.'

'So, what?' said West. 'Another insurance scam?'

'No, nothing was stolen. I'm thinking life assurance, maybe. And see here, the way Eileen Hunter took herself off to Mallorca while her husband was in hospital, that's not right, is it? If you asked me, I'd say she knew what was going to happen and got herself out of the way.'

'Well, if you're right,' said West, 'then maybe that's enough to get her back.'

'And if it's not?'

'Then we're caught between the devil and the deep blue sea. Short of hopping on a plane, there's not much else we can do.'

'There is one thing,' said Dougal. 'Something that could bolster our case.'

'What's that then?'

'She's not here, is she? The house is empty. They must have records or documents or emails about their insurance or pensions lying about the place. If we could find out how much Ross Hunter was worth then maybe we're in with a shout.'

'You,' said West, 'are on top form, and as this is now a murder inquiry, it's no holds barred. We'll shoot over there in a bit and have a good shufty round.'

* * *

Despite the heat and weight of his leather jacket, Duncan, looking as cool as a cucumber, strolled into the office and made a bee-line for the bag on the desk.

'Who the hell eats chicken wraps?' he said. 'Is somebody on a diet?'

'Actually, they're not bad,' said Dougal. 'You should try one.'

'I'd rather boil my head. Thanks, miss, you're a saviour.'

'No worries,' said West, 'it's probably cold by now.'

'I'm not fussed, it'll warm up once I've swallowed it.'

'Are you all sorted?'

'Aye, I've sent Meena's gear to forensics in Glasgow,' said Duncan, 'and I've asked them to fast-track it. Once I get this down my neck, I'll have a chat with Navinder. Has he been booked in?'

'He has,' said Dougal. 'His details are being processed as we speak, we should be live in about an hour.'

'Magic. A wee favour then, pal. Once he's on the system, can you run a cross-match for me? We need to know if his prints match those on the knife we got from the restaurant.'

'No bother.'

'So, what about you, miss?' said Duncan as he polished off the fries. 'What's your next move?'

'We're on our way out again,' said West. 'Hunter's gaff in Troon, we're going to have a mooch around.'

'We?' said Dougal, a look of disappointment on his face. 'Oh, I'm not sure about that, miss. I've a heap of stuff to get through here.'

'It was your idea, sunshine, and you could do with some vitamin D, you're looking as white as a sheet.'

'Oh, you may as well leave him be,' said Duncan. 'If you pop him in the sun, he's liable to wilt. I'll come, if you like.'

'What about Navinder?'

'We've plenty of time. Another hour or two won't hurt.'

'Okay,' said West, 'get one of the lads downstairs to follow us, we'll need the big key to get in.'

'We'll not need to bust his door down; I'll get us in, no bother, but we should take my motor.'

'Yours?' said West. 'What's wrong with mine?'

'That ropey old Defender? No offence, miss, but we don't want to draw attention to ourselves.'

'That's rich, coming from you,' said West. 'Have you looked in a mirror lately?'

Chapter 18

Set in the vicinity of a golf course, a luxury hotel, and for the increasingly frail, a private nursing home, the secluded and sparsely populated Southwood Road – cutting a discreet swathe through the Ayrshire countryside – was the perfect location for wealthy business types who, rather than mingle with the hoi-polloi, chose to avoid their neighbours, receive callers by appointment only, and secrete their fleets of luxury vehicles in chalet-style garages large enough to house a family of twelve.

Hidden by a crop of unruly leylandii to the front and bounded by woodland to the rear, the Hunters' residence – a comparatively modest affair with a landscaped lawn, a paved patio, and an ornamental pond brimming with Coy carp – was sheltered enough to protect its occupants from the inquisitive gaze of curious passers-by.

Duncan stepped from the car and, craning his neck to the roof, inspected the front of the property.

'No sign of any alarms,' he said, as he wandered to the rear.

'They might have one of those fancy, silent types,' said West, 'you know, with a relay signal that goes straight to a call centre.'

'No, I'm not convinced,' said Duncan. 'I'd expect to see security cameras by the points of entry if they had a set-up like that. No, no, I think we'll be okay.'

'Well, I hope you're right. The last thing we need right now is Plod storming up the path.'

'Oh, we can handle them, no bother.'

'Okay, so how are we getting in?'

Duncan pulled Munro's small leather pouch from his jacket pocket and winked.

'Just call me Raffles,' he said.

'You're going to get us into trouble, you know that?'

'How so?' said Duncan indignantly. 'I'm saving the force a repair bill, they're not cheap, new doors. Especially timber ones like this.'

'Well, at least it's not one of those horrible plastic jobbies everyone seems to have these days.'

Duncan dropped to his knees, took two pins from the pouch and, after much wiggling, poking, and cursing under his breath, finally tripped the lock.

'Dear, dear, dear,' he said. 'It's only a three-lever mortice. I'm not sure their insurance company would be happy about that.'

West stepped inside, placed her hands on her hips and, with a disparaging shake of the head, surveyed the large, fully-fitted kitchen replete with flagstones, two double ovens, a built-in microwave, and a refectory table surrounded by six leather-backed chairs.

'You're not seriously telling me someone actually lives here?' she said. 'Look at the place, it's immaculate.'

'Maybe they have a cleaner.'

'Either that, or they eat out seven days a week. Honestly, just look at it, it's soulless. I mean, we're talking zero personality here.'

'Just like Eileen Hunter.'

'Now, now. That's enough of that. Come on, we'll start at the top and work our way down.'

Duncan sprinted up the stairs, paused on the landing, and counted the doors along the hallway while he waited for West to catch up.

'I've stayed in hotels with fewer rooms than this,' he said. 'Not as clean, mind, I'll give you that.'

'I think you're confusing the word "hotel" with "hostel",' said West. 'This way.'

The two opposing rooms at the end of the hall – minimally furnished with matching steel-frame beds, flat-pack wardrobes, and bedside tables – were clearly set aside for the use of guests, although, mused West as she ran a finger through the dust on the window ledge, visitors to the house were clearly few and far between.

The adjacent bathroom, similarly Scandinavian in style, was home to a single hand towel, a bar of soap, and a mirrored wall cabinet containing precisely one razor, one packet of razor blades, and a can of shaving foam.

'She must have packed all her stuff and taken it with her,' said West.

'If she did,' said Duncan, 'she's not fussed about shaving her legs. The thing is, miss, it's not making sense. I mean, why would she take all her toiletries with her? Surely she'd have all she needs at her place in Santa Ponsa?'

'I think you might be right,' said West as she slipped next door, 'look at this, separate bathrooms.'

'I'm not surprised,' said Duncan, 'if I was Ross Hunter, I'd insist on it. The place is a tip.'

'It's what we women like to call "organised chaos".'

'It's what I'd call slatternly. Why does one woman need so much make-up, anyway? She has enough here to open a market stall.'

'A word of advice,' said West, 'never ask a woman what she needs or why, or you'll end up single in no time.'

Bypassing the closet and a utility cupboard, the two remaining rooms on the upper level were, like the bathrooms, 'his and hers'.

Rumpled bed aside, 'his' was neatly appointed with a wardrobe full of pressed chinos and striped shirts, a silver alarm clock, and an array of framed photographs featuring a small boy, some with and some without his mother; whilst 'hers', bereft of any personal items, had all the charm of a Travelodge.

Scooting around the study on a desk chair like a wean on bring-your-kid-to-work day, West pondered the state of the Hunters' personal relationship while Duncan, snapping on a pair of gloves, perused the well-stocked bookshelves.

'So, they're obviously leading separate lives,' she said. 'Separate bedrooms, separate bathrooms.'

'Aye, and by the looks of it,' said Duncan, 'she probably hogs the telly in the lounge while he hides himself away in here. This is all, dare I say it, lads' stuff.'

'I wonder how long they've been living apart, so to speak?'

'That all depends on when she gave up cleaning the bathroom,' said Duncan as he pulled a yellow box file from the shelf. 'I think I've just found the business section of his library.'

'What have you got?'

'Paperwork. This is full of renewals for their insurance policies. Buildings, contents, car, public liability, professional indemnity, stock. He's well-covered, I'll give him that.'

'Doesn't surprise me, he's probably desperate to keep his nose clean after torching their place in Edinburgh.'

'To be fair, we still don't know for sure if it was Ross who did it,' said Duncan as he handed West another file. 'Here, take a look in that.'

'Receipts,' said West, 'and invoices. Suppliers and wholesalers by the looks of it. You?'

'I think this one should be marked "motive". These are annual statements from his pension providers.'

'Providers? Plural?'

'Aye, four of them,' said Duncan. 'Aviva, Scottish Widows, Royal London, and Fidelity.'

'That's irony for you.'

'How so?'

'Widows and fidelity. So, was he worth bumping off?'

'I'd say so, aye. He's had these going for twenty years or more, and he's been paying three hundred pounds into each one religiously every month.'

'Twelve hundred quid a month into a flipping pension? He must be earning a fortune! So, what's he worth?'

'Well,' said Duncan, waving a sheet of paper, 'this one alone has a transfer value of £198,000.'

'Bloody nora!' said West. 'So, roughly speaking, he's worth about a million, then?'

'More, I'd say, especially if he's dead. Don't forget he's got life assurance on top of this. And his state pension, too.'

'Cripes,' said West, pointing towards his computer. 'I bet that Eileen Hunter's got her eye on a yacht already. Boot that up, would you? Let's see what he's been up to.'

Duncan fired up the desktop, stood back, and shook his head as a flowery icon appeared in the centre of the screen.

'Windows 7,' he said. 'And without a password, we're humped.'

'Poppycock,' said West. 'Bag it up. Dougal'll be running around inside that thing before we even get our coats off.'

Chapter 19

Unlike his parents, who excelled in the art of raising their voices until neither could be heard, Duncan was wise enough to realise that in any relationship, be it personal or professional, there were times, arguments and grudges aside, when the unexpected and often protracted silence of a particular individual was to be respected lest a barrage of questions concerning the cause of their angst compel them to commit an act of grievous bodily harm.

With nothing to accompany them but the roar of the wind as it blasted through the open windows, Duncan, wary of disturbing the peace, gently floored the Audi while West, her mind as addled as a multi-tasker with Alzheimer's, sat in quiet contemplation all the way back to the office.

* * *

'Are you okay?' said Dougal as they strolled through the door. 'Or did somebody give you a vegan sausage roll?'

'Don't ask,' said West as she flicked on the kettle, 'just get ready with a pad and pencil.'

'How was it? The Hunters', I mean?'

'Well, they share the same house but that's about it. They may as well be flatmates.'

'Some folk like it like that,' said Dougal. 'It helps to keep the spark alive.'

'Well, they'd have to plug in to the national grid if they've any chance of re-igniting that spark, I can tell you. Any word from Jimbo, yet?'

'No, miss. Not a dickie bird. Why?'

'No reason,' said West, 'except he's been gone ages, and it's getting late, that's all.'

'He was okay when I left him,' said Duncan, 'trust me. He'll be fine.'

'You say that, but in this heat, after his operation.'

'Look, the worst that could possibly happen is that they let the dog go free and lock the chief in the pound. He'll be in touch when he's ready. Besides, he was going shopping anyway.'

'Shopping?'

'Aye, he was after a few bits and bobs for the wean, I mean, dog.'

'Okay,' said West, 'if he's not back by the time we knock off, I'll give him a bell. Right, back to business. Dougal, first task, I want to know if either Ross or Eileen Hunter were having an affair.'

'An affair!' said Dougal. 'So, you think Ross Hunter's death could have been a crime of passion, then?'

'No, love's got nothing to do with it.'

'I disagree,' said Duncan. 'Eileen Hunter has a love of money.'

'True,' said West, 'and as we're on the subject, did you have any luck with Ross Hunter's bank account?'

'Aye, I did,' said Dougal, 'but there's not much to get excited about, just a load of direct debits, standing orders, and cash withdrawals.'

'Cash? How much?'

'Peanuts. Fifty quid here and there.'

'Bugger. So, not enough to keep Peggy McClure in clover, then. Okay, next thing, I need you to do the same with Eileen Hunter. I want anything you can find regarding her financial situation. What we really need to know is whether she was desperate enough to kill her husband so she could get her hands on his cash, or if she has enough to get by on her own.'

'No bother,' said Dougal, 'I've already got her bank details so we're halfway there.'

'How'd you get that?'

'There's a direct debit set up from their business account, she's been taking two grand a month.'

'And I bet she hasn't paid a penny in tax,' said West.

'I can find that out, too,' said Dougal. 'Okay, that's plenty to keep me busy for now.'

'Sorry, pal,' said Duncan as he hauled the computer onto the desk, 'one more thing, we need to get inside this, and we need you to have a nosey around.'

Dougal leapt from his seat and, like a child with a new toy, eagerly wired-up a monitor, plugged it in, and sighed with disappointment as the screen burst into life.

'Oh, don't tell me you can't do it,' said Duncan. 'Do you not have any of that clever hacking software?'

'You mean like "Ophcrack", or "Brutus"? Of course I do, aye, but I'll not need it.'

'Then why the face?'

'Because it's old system software,' said Dougal as he restarted the computer, 'it's not much of a challenge. I can simply log-in as "administrator". Look, you just hit F8 while it's starting up; that takes you to the boot menu, we choose "safe mode" like this, click "enter", and log-in as administrator. Done.'

'Jeez-oh,' said Duncan. 'And you can do that with any computer?'

'If it's running Windows 8 or before, aye. Now all we have to do is click "start", go to the control panel, and we can change the password to anything we like. Easy. So, what are we after?'

'Hunter was loaded,' said West, 'we know that because we found his pension statements but we need to find out who the beneficiary is on all his investments.'

'Would that not be his next of kin?'

'Not necessarily.'

'Okay,' said Dougal, 'unless I can access it online, I might have to make a few phone calls once I've found the relevant paperwork. Leave me to it.'

'Oh, just a thought,' said West, 'see if you can find a last will and testament, too. You never know, if he had the foresight to make one, it might throw up a few clues. So, that's us taken care of, what have you been up to?'

Dougal, whizzing around the PC with the laid-back nonchalance of a jaded video-gamer, reeled off a progress report as if reciting a verse he'd learned off pat.

'Uniform have got a still off the camera at the jewellers,' he said, 'they're calling on all the Aygo owners as we speak. FS in Glasgow came back with the test results on the gear from Tarif Khan's flat. It's clean; nothing but traces of Khan himself there. And McLeod's been asking for you.'

'Andy?' said West, her face dropping. 'What does he want? Don't tell me he's still hankering after that drink?'

'I've no idea,' said Dougal, 'but he did ask for you to call him back. Oh, and he mentioned Khan, too. He said the fingers were his, no doubt about it.'

'Well, there's a surprise, I mean, they're hardly likely to belong to somebody else now, are they?'

'Right,' said Duncan, 'that's me away. I'll leave you to organise your love-life in peace. I'm going to have a wee chat with Navinder.'

'Hold fire!' said Dougal. 'Do you not want some ammo?'

'Ammo?'

'Aye, that knife from the Punjabi Grill, the blade's got Tarif Khan's DNA all over it, which proves beyond a shadow of a doubt that it was used to amputate his fingers.'

'That's smashing,' said Duncan, 'but it's not going to nail Navinder Singh-Gill as the perpetrator, is it?'

'No, but the fact it has his fingerprints all over the handle *will*.'

* * *

Slouching in his seat with his hands in his pockets and his legs splayed apart, Navinder Singh-Gill, a cocksure scally with scant regard for the law, smirked as he locked eyes with Duncan who, dispensing with pleasantries, tucked his chair beneath the desk, stabbed the voice recorder, and leant against the wall.

'I'm DS Reid,' he said. 'For the benefit of the tape, would you please state your name.'

'Nav.'

'Your full name.'

'Navinder Singh-Gill.'

'Okay. Just for the record, you're not under arrest and you've not been charged. You've attended voluntarily under suspicion of assault and you're under no obligation to say anything other than to provide your name, your date of birth, nationality, and your address. Do you understand?'

Navinder smiled smugly and nodded.

'Sounds like a deal,' he said.

'Good. I've a few questions about a pal of yours, a Mr Tarif Khan.'

'He's not my pal.'

'But you know each other?'

'Aye.'

'It sounds to me like you don't get on.'

'We get on,' said Navinder. 'Well enough.'

'But he's not your pal?'

'No. he's Ash's…'

'Ash's what?' said Duncan. 'Friend? Or should I say, boyfriend?'

Navinder looked to the floor and grimaced.

'I seem to have touched a nerve,' said Duncan. 'Have you something against Tarif?'

'No.'

'Have you something against homosexuals, then?'

'I've nothing against anyone,' said Navinder. 'Each to his own.'

'If you say so. I hear you had a wee party at your place not so long ago. Just you and your brother, his pal, and your stepsister. Is that right?'

'It wasn't a party, it was just the four of us, a few family drinks, that's all.'

'But you had a good night?'

'It was nothing special,' said Navinder. 'Like I said, a few bevvies, that's all it was.'

'So, you weren't up till the wee hours annoying the neighbours with your music?'

'No.'

'And what about Meena? Did she enjoy herself?'

'I suppose so.'

'That's not what I heard,' said Duncan, 'I heard she was that bored, she took herself off to bed.'

'That's not true. She was hammered.'

'Hammered? Is she fond of her drink, then?'

'She likes a drop, aye. But she can't handle it.'

'So with Meena away in her bed, it was just the three of you, was it? You, Ash, and Tarif?'

Navinder crossed his arms, pursed his lips, and nodded.

'That's right, just the three us.'

'That's odd,' said Duncan, 'because your brother, see, he says he and Tarif took themselves off to the pub soon after Meena went to her bed. Why is that? Why would they leave if you were all having such a good time?'

'Search me,' said Navinder. 'Maybe they got bored.'

'Aye. Maybe. Or maybe it's because a couple of uninvited guests turned up.'

'Guests?'

'Aye, two fellas,' said Duncan. 'Pals of yours. I hear they started intimidating Ash and Tarif.'

'They were not intimidating anyone, they were…'

'Dear, dear, dear,' said Duncan, 'you really need to watch yourself, Nav, that's the second time you've tripped yourself up and we've not even been here that long. So, these two fellas, who were they?'

'Just a couple of lads from the pub.'

'And did you invite them?'

'Aye. No.'

'Which is it?'

'No.'

'So they didn't stay?'

'No, I sent them on their way.'

'And when did they leave? Was it before or after Ash and Tarif?'

'I don't remember.'

'No. Of course you don't,' said Duncan. 'Tell me, how long have you and Meena been living together? Under the same roof, I mean.'

'Ever since my dad got wed.'

'And you get along okay?'

'Aye. Okay.'

Duncan stepped forward, perched himself on the edge of the desk, and lowered his voice.

'She's quite a looker,' he said with a crafty grin. 'In fact, I'd go so far as to say, she's actually quite stunning.'

'I've never noticed.'

'Never noticed! You need an eye test, pal! Are you telling me, you don't fancy her?'

'She's alright.'

'So you do?'

'I mean, she's alright.'

'Have you got a girlfriend, yourself?'

'That's none of your business.'

'Oh, that's where you're wrong, pal,' said Duncan. 'See here, everything's my business, right down to what you had for breakfast, so I'll ask you again, do you have a girlfriend?'

'No comment.'

'What about your two pals? Are they single, too?'

'No comment.'

Content to accept that the arrogance of youth was not a trait confined to his generation, Duncan, smiling softly to himself, ambled along the side of the room until he slipped from Khan's line of sight.

'You're not like your brother, are you?' he said. 'Ash is actually a decent fella. He's not into lies or deception, or thieving or violence. He's honest, and he likes to look out for folk too. Like Meena, he treats her like a real sister, flesh and blood. He's got her back, and she respects him for that. She *confides* in him.'

Duncan approached Navinder, stopped beside him, and paused before leaning into his ear.

'See here, Nav,' he said, his voice barely more than a whisper. 'I know what happened that night. I know what happened to Meena. And I know for a fact that you and your two pals were alone in the house with her. So, here's the deal. You can either tell me who they are, or you're going to take the fall for the assault. Do I make myself clear?'

Navinder, squirming in his seat, cleared his throat and wiped his dry lips with the palm of his hand.

'I don't know what you're talking about,' he said. 'I don't know what happened to Meena.'

'Is that so? Well, maybe you know what happened to Tarif, then.'

'Surprise me.'

'He lost all his fingers.'

Drained of the streetwise bravado that gave him a sense of invincibility amongst the neds and chancers of

136

Ayrshire's less salubrious pubs and clubs, Navinder lowered his head and began to snigger.

'He should have been more careful,' he said, nervously.

'No, no,' said Duncan. 'You see, Nav, it's you who should have been more careful.'

'How so?'

'We've got your prints all over the knife that was used in the assault on Tarif Khan.'

'Away! If you're so clever, tell me where you found this knife!'

'In your restaurant, the Punjabi Grill.'

'Well, what do you expect!' said Navinder. 'I work there! They would be!'

'Sorry, pal, but the game's a bogey. The only question is, why? Why did you do it?'

'No comment.'

'You're hanging yourself, here,' said Duncan. 'See, Nav, if you tell us why you did it, then they may show you some leniency when you appear in court.'

'Court?'

'Aye. Last chance.'

'No comment.'

'Then you leave me no choice,' said Duncan, returning to the desk. 'Navinder Singh-Gill, I'm going to charge you but before I do, I must caution you that you do not need to say anything in answer to the charge, but anything you do say will be noted and may be used in evidence. Do you understand?'

'Get it up you!'

'The charge against you is that you did commit an act of GBH with intent against Tarif Khan.'

'You are joking me, right?'

'I'm also charging you with possession of an offensive weapon.'

'I'm a Sikh!' said Navinder. 'I'm allowed to carry a kirpan!'

'Dear, oh dear, you've done it again,' said Duncan. 'Who said anything about a kirpan? Now, do you have anything to say in reply to the charge? No? Then let's get you swabbed and printed; you'll be in court first thing tomorrow morning.'

* * *

Although the weight of the evidence would doubtless see Navinder Singh-Gill serving a custodial sentence for the assault on Tarif Khan, Duncan, assessing his juvenile display of machismo as an antic more worthy of the playground rather than the underworld, deemed him incapable of committing such a crime unless he'd acted under duress, an opinion which also called into question his culpability concerning the rape of his stepsister.

Perturbed by the lack of a motive, he stopped halfway up the stairwell, sat down, and telephoned Navinder's brother.

'Ash,' he said. 'It's DS Reid. Are you okay, pal?'

'Hello, Sergeant. Aye, not bad. What's occurring?'

'I've a wee bit of bad news for you. Your brother, Nav, he's just been charged with assault.'

'On Tarif?'

'Aye. GBH with intent. He'll be in court tomorrow and there's no doubt he'll be banged up for a while, so you might want to tell your folks.'

'They'll not be happy,' said Ash. 'Mind you, they'll not be sad, either.'

'How so?'

'They believe in the letter of the law, Sergeant. They'll be the first to say, lock him up and don't let him out until he's seen sense.'

'And you?'

'He'll get what he deserves.'

'Fair enough,' said Duncan. 'Listen, Ash, I could do with some help.'

'I'll do my best.'

'I need you to have a word with Meena.'

'Meena? What about?'

'We need a swab so we can get a sample of her DNA. It's not an intrusive procedure, just a wee cotton bud on the inside of her cheek, the whole thing takes two seconds.'

'I don't know if she'll agree to that,' said Ash. 'She hasn't so far.'

'That's why I need you to convince her that it's the right thing to do. Look, she's already given us her bed sheets from the night of the attack. If we do find any DNA on them, then we have to be sure it's not hers, and we can't do that unless we have her on the database. Do you get what I'm saying?'

'Aye, of course, but you know how stubborn she can be. I'll have a word, but don't hold your breath.'

'Smashing. Now, one more thing: it's about the two fellas who gatecrashed your party.'

'Oh, I'm not sure about that, Sergeant,' said Ash, 'you see...'

'Look, there's no point in covering for them, we need to know...'

'It's not that. I just don't know anything about them.'

'Nothing?' said Duncan. 'Nothing at all? Not even a name? Or an address, maybe?'

'Nothing.'

'How about where they work?'

'Sorry.'

'Okay, a description, then?'

'Oh, aye,' said Ash, 'now that, I can help you with. One fella's a short-arse, about five-feet, five. He's fat, with a big beer belly, and he's thin on top.'

'And the other?'

'The opposite. He's about the same height as you, slim but not skinny, and he's got brown hair.'

'That's cracking, Ash. Now, have you any idea where I can find them? Where they hang out?'

'The only place I can think of is Nav's local, that's where he used to meet them. The Redstone Inn, it's over in Heathfield.'

'Heathfield? Is that not a bit far for a local?'

'Aye, but Nav likes it there, only because he can stop for fried chicken on the way home without taking a detour.'

'Fair enough, I'll pop over in a couple of minutes.'

'You'll be wasting your time,' said Ash, 'they'll not be there now.'

'How so?'

'It's only Thursday, Friday's the day they get hammered; they work a half day.'

Chapter 20

'Heigh-ho,' said Duncan, rubbing his eyes as he trudged into the office, 'it's quiet in here.'

'We've been busy,' said West, peering over her laptop. 'Bloody hell, you look like I feel.'

'You should get yourself to the hospital, then.'

'What's the score?'

'Police Scotland-1, Criminals-0. I've done him for GBH with intent. All I have to do now is get a report ready for the fiscal.'

'No bother,' said Dougal. 'You look done in; I'll sort it.'

'Are you sure?'

'Aye, it won't take long. Besides, I could do with a break, I've had it up to the back teeth looking at how much folk are worth, dead or alive.'

'You'll not have that problem with me,' said Duncan, 'I'm worthless whichever way you look at it.'

'Did you get anywhere with the assault on Meena?' said West. 'I'm assuming if you've done him for GBH then he's not said anything about the rape?'

'Not a sausage,' said Duncan, 'but I got the distinct impression he was covering for the two lads who showed up at their house.'

'Why would he do that?'

'Who knows? He was cagey about them, though; just rattled off a string of "no comments" every time I mentioned them. It's almost as though they have some sort of a hold on him.'

'Well, if they have,' said West, 'it must be something big if he's that scared of them.'

'Oh, it wouldn't take much to scare Navinder Singh-Gill,' said Duncan, 'he's all mouth and no trousers, which is why…'

'Why what?'

Duncan pulled up a chair, took a deep breath, and sighed as he propped his feet on the desk.

'Frankly, miss, I just don't think he's got it in him. He's just not a rapist. And Meena is his sister after all. Stepsister, I'll give you that, but all the same.'

'So, you reckon it was one of these blokes, then?'

'Has to be,' said Duncan, 'but all we have to go on is a description from Ash, and the name of their local. I'm going to nip over there tomorrow evening to see if I can spot them.'

'Well, make sure you keep a low profile, you don't want to scare them off.'

'No danger of that,' said Dougal, 'the only problem he'll have is getting served. A lot of pubs have a dress code these days.'

'I'll dress you in a minute. So, what are you two up to?'

'Nothing anymore,' said West, 'I don't know about you, Dougal, but I've had enough. I still haven't heard a peep from Jimbo so I'm going to give him a call when I get home.'

'I'm stopping here a while,' said Dougal. 'As soon as I've done the report for the fiscal, I want to have a sniff around Eileen Hunter.'

'I'd not say that in public,' said Duncan, 'or you'll give folk the wrong idea.'

West closed her computer, grabbed her coat, and froze momentarily as the unmistakable sound of DCI Elliot's dulcet tones boomed along the corridor.

'Charlie! Are you there? Charlie! Where the devil are you?'

'Right, that's me away!' said Duncan as he raced towards the back door.

'Hold up!' said West, 'I'm coming with you.'

'Charlie! Do you not have a minute to…?'

Elliot's words tailed off as he appeared in the doorway, scowling as he surveyed the empty office.

'Dougal!' he said. 'Where on earth has she gone?'

'Oh, she's on a shout, sir. With Duncan. They'll not be back tonight.'

'Hell and damnation! Oh, well, tomorrow it is, then.'

'Can you not just give her call?'

'No, no. What I have to say has to be done face to face.'

'Oh, dear.'

'When you see her, tell her she's to stay put until she's spoken to me, do I make myself clear?'

* * *

Dismissing the results of a poll that cited freshly-baked bread, coffee, and cut grass as the nation's favourite smells, West, who considered the findings nothing more than an underhand ploy to boost the sales of flour, yeast, and lawnmowers, preferred the distinctive aroma of a volatile vindaloo, the welcoming whiff of a pan-fried steak, and the unmistakable odour of a dripping pump at a petrol station.

Acutely aware of a presence in her apartment, she tossed her coat to the floor and, expecting to find Munro busying himself in the kitchen, made her way down the hall, her nose twitching against the unexpected and less than desirable niff of a musty, woodland walk.

'Charlie! You're back!'

'And where the hell have you been?' said West. 'I've been worried sick! I thought you might have snuffed it behind the wheel and careered into a ditch.'

'Well, as you can see, I'm very much alive, and exceedingly well. And for your delectation, I've taken the liberty of preparing us a celebratory supper,' said Munro.

'In that case, you're forgiven. I've had a right day of it and I'm flipping starving. What are we having?'

'Two prime cuts of dry-aged, fillet steak.'

'Don't think me rude,' said West, 'I mean, no offence, Jimbo, but they smell a bit off.'

'It's not the steak, Charlie,' said Munro as he nodded towards the sofa behind her, 'it's the cause of our celebration.'

West slowly turned and caught sight of a small, jet-black Scottish Terrier sitting on the couch, his tail banging rhythmically against the cushions.

'Oh! My! God!' she said as she dashed towards him. 'He's adorable! Blooming heck, Jimbo, he's humming.'

'Aye, well, it's to be expected. After all, the poor chap's been cooped up in kennels for some weeks, now. We'll throw him in the tub when we've finished our supper.'

'What's he called?'

'Murdo.'

'Good. Well, I'll sit here with Murdo while you fetch me some vino.'

Munro poured two large glasses of red, took a sip from one, and passed the other to West along with a dog biscuit.

'That's not an Italian snack,' he said. 'It's for Murdo.'

'Very funny. So, how are you? Are you feeling okay?'

'Aye, Charlie, why wouldn't I be?'

'I'm just checking. I know what you're like; you could have a ten-inch blade sticking out of your chest and you'd still say "I'm fine".'

'Well, I am,' said Munro. 'In fact, I'm better than fine. You sit there with that wee man on your lap and tell me you're not overcome with a positive sense of well-being.'

'I don't have to,' said West. 'I was brought up with them. Springers and Labs, mainly.'

'Ah, the trappings of the privileged classes. Did you not have a wee horse in the stables, too?'

'Shut it.'

'So,' said Munro as he oiled the steaks and popped them in the pan, 'are you making progress?'

'Of sorts,' said West. 'Navinder Singh-Gill's all but banged up, he won't see daylight for a while, but Duncan's having doubts about his involvement with the rape.'

'You do surprise me. I was under the impression the fellow was alone in the house with that young lady.'

'So were we,' said West, 'but no. Apparently, there were two other geezers in the house as well. Both uninvited. Duncan's going to see if he can track them down tomorrow.'

'Well, if anyone can find them, Duncan can. He has a talent for going unnoticed amongst society's more unsavoury characters.'

'Apart from that, I've spent most of the day with Dougal trying to establish a motive for the attack on Ross Hunter, and at the moment it's looking more and more like that old chestnut – money.'

'Ah, the root of all evil,' said Munro. 'And the branches. So, you're not of the opinion the assailant himself was after his cash?'

'No. I reckon he was just the hired help. I think someone put him up to it.'

'And who would that be?'

'God knows,' said West, 'but everything seems to be pointing towards his wife, purely because she legged it to Santa Ponsa soon after it happened, and she's probably the only one who knows exactly what he's worth.'

West drained her glass and waved it at Munro.

'The problem is, Jimbo, there's just one tiny thing that's niggling me.'

'It's the niggles that keep you on your toes, Charlie. Go on.'

'Well, it's completely unrelated but I was at the recycling centre having a natter with Peggy McClure and her mate came over. A bloke by the name of Miller, he's the one who was with her when they pulled the fingers out of the rubbish.'

'And?'

'Well, we had a brief chat,' said West, 'nothing major, just niceties really, and Peggy said to him *"I've told her everything she needs to know"* and he said, *"not everything I hope".'*

'Is that it?'

'Yeah. Don't you think it's a bit odd?'

'Not particularly,' said Munro as he pulled the chips from the oven. 'It sounds like a wee bit of friendly banter to me.'

'That's what I thought,' said West, 'apart from one thing. He winked when he said it.'

'At her?'

'Yeah, but it wasn't like a jokey, nudge-nudge, kind of a wink; it was sly, like I wasn't meant to see it.'

'And what does your gut tell you?'

'I'm not sure,' said West, 'but I can't help thinking there's something going on between them.'

'Then perhaps,' said Munro, 'you need to ask her up front. Or perhaps you should let them get on with their lives. They're two grown adults, Charlie. What they get up to in private is their business, not yours. Now, give your head a break and let's eat.'

West, struggling to remove Murdo from her lap, carried him to the table and set him on the floor.

'Just a moment,' said Munro as he fetched a bowl from the counter. 'This wee man needs his supper, too.'

'Don't tell me he's having steak, as well?'

'I'm not made of money, lassie. No, no, he's having some grain-free, organic food made with grass-fed lamb and peas.'

'Did you get him a high-chair so he can join us at the table?'

'No,' said Munro, 'but there's a high-jump outside and you'll be heading for it if you're not careful. Okay, back to Eileen Hunter, it sounds as though you've not got very far.'

'We haven't,' said West, 'I mean, we're getting there but the bottom line is we just don't have enough on her yet to nick her for anything, let alone request a warrant to bring her back, but Dougal's on the case. He's ferreting around her finances as we speak so I'm hoping he'll have something by the morning.'

'Well, it's the wean I feel sorry for,' said Munro as he tucked into his steak. 'His father's dead and his mother's away on her holidays, it cannae be easy for the lad.'

'You'd have thought so,' said West, 'but according to Dougal he sounded surprisingly upbeat.'

'Is that so? Then perhaps the fact that he's not seen his family in a while is making the trauma that much easier to bear.'

'That's what Duncan said. Anyway, apparently Kieran gave Dougal the third degree when he spoke to him. A hundred and one questions about the nature of his work – had he caught any bank robbers or serial killers – you know, the usual thing. He was even polite enough to ask after Peggy McClure.'

'McClure?'

'Yup. Like I said, she must have had quite an influence on him.'

'But he's not seen her in years.'

'I know!' said West. 'Amazing, isn't it? Mind you, she did look after him, and she was the one who encouraged his painting, and all that. What's up? You're not having a turn, are you?'

'No, no,' said Munro, 'it's simply what the medical profession refer to as acute instinctitus.'

'You what?'

'See here, Charlie, I'm not a parent. Never have been, never will be, but it strikes me that a child, regardless of his situation, would be more inclined to enquire after the welfare of his mother than a teacher he's not seen since school.'

'Maybe he had a crush on her.'

Munro raised his eyebrows, pushed his plate to one side and, topping up their glasses, chuckled to himself.

'What are you snickering at?' said West.

'Come come, Charlie. Look, I know you've had a long day, and I know you've had a wee drink, but it's not that difficult really, is it?'

West, her eyes slowly widening, glared across the table, pulled her phone from her hip and bolted to the balcony while Murdo, aroused by the smell of the food, pawed at Munro before wandering to the kitchen in search of anything that may have dropped to the floor.

* * *

'I'm not one to pry,' said Munro as West, looking befuddled, returned to the room, 'but that call…'

'You know damn well who I just called. I swear to God, I don't know how you do it. I really don't.'

'Come, come. Dinnae denigrate yourself, Charlie, sometimes it's easy to overlook the obvious.'

'Well, you were right,' said West. 'It turns out Ross Hunter was never alone when he went to Lathallan. He always had company. Peggy McClure.'

'Then you appear to have something of a dilemma on your hands.'

'How d'you figure that?'

'Well,' said Munro, 'you suspect McClure of being in cahoots with this Miller chap but in fact she appears to have been involved with Hunter as well.'

'Nothing wrong with her libido, then, is there?' said West as she cleared the table.

'Of course,' said Munro, 'there is the possibility that both of these relationships are quite above board. The question is... what do you plan to do about it?'

West piled the plates in the sink and stared blankly at the floor.

'I think we need to call Taggart,' she said.

'Taggart?'

'There's been a Murdo in the kitchen.'

Munro, not given to hysterical bouts of laughter, howled with delight as he rose to his feet.

'It's probably first night nerves,' he said, reaching for the Balvenie. 'Give me a moment, Charlie, and I'll clear it up.'

Chapter 21

Prone to blaming his failures on ineptitude rather than a lack of facts, clues, or even circumstantial evidence, Dougal, looking as glum as a grouse on the Glorious Twelfth, set about widening his search for the elusive hatchback by trawling the dealerships for any recent acquisitions, and the council records for any which may have been ticketed, towed, or abandoned.

'Morning all,' said West as she breezed into the office. 'Where's Duncan?'

'Café.'

'Excellent. You look happy, what's rattled your cage?'

'Everything,' said Dougal. 'It seems I was wrong about the Aygo, miss. Uniform drew a complete blank. Not one single household recognised the fella on the still.'

'Och, you cannae blame yourself for that,' said Munro. 'That was simply one line of inquiry that you had to follow through. Now, check it off your list and move on to the next one.'

'Jimbo's right,' said West. 'Don't tell me you've been moping about it all night long?'

'No, no. I've been too busy.'

'Well then,' said Munro, 'there's nothing to be morose about. Here, perhaps this fellow will cheer you up.'

'Jeez-oh!' said Dougal. 'Is that a dog?'

'I believe so.'

'Why is he staring at me?'

'He can smell fear.'

'Does he bite?'

'Only if he's hungry.'

'Well, if it's all the same with you,' said Dougal, 'I'd rather you kept him over there, I'm not that good with dogs.'

'I am,' said Duncan as he dumped a carrier bag on the desk. 'Breakfast all round, help yourselves. Sorry, chief, if I'd known your sidekick was joining us, I'd have fetched him something too.'

'Much appreciated,' said Munro, 'but he's had his. If he gets peckish, he can have a wee nibble on young Dougal, there.'

'Right then,' said West, 'as we're all here, I'll stick the kettle on while he tells us what's been happening on the night shift.'

'Right you are,' said Dougal. 'I'll start with Eileen Hunter. Financially speaking, the way things stand, I'd say she's comfortable enough by anyone's standards. She has a few grand in her current account here, and she has a sizeable stash in an account with the Banco Sabadell in Palma.'

'Palma? How the hell did you find that out?'

'Easy. She's been transferring funds from their business account for some years now.'

'So,' said Duncan, 'the bottom line is, she's not skint, and she's not desperate.'

'Right enough,' said Dougal, 'but with her husband dead and no income to speak of, it's not going to last long.'

'What are you thinking, Jimbo?' said West as she tore into a sausage sandwich. 'You're looking confused.'

'I'm not confused, lassie. I'm cogitating. You see, Charlie, the only reason she could possibly have for wanting to realise his assets, is if she knew he was going to die and their business was going to go down the pan. Even then, as the likely beneficiary, you have to ask yourself the question, would it have been necessary to kill her husband?'

'Maybe,' said West, 'if she wanted to get her hands on the money quick. I mean, otherwise she could have been waiting another twenty or thirty years.'

'Well, that's assuming,' said Munro, 'that she was behind the attack on her husband; in other words, that the whole sorry affair was premeditated.'

'Well, yeah. Of course.'

'But what if she wasnae behind the attack? If that's so, then you'll have to find another suspect.'

'Thanks,' said West, 'I'll put an ad in the paper, shall I?'

Duncan rose from his chair, relieved Munro of the dog, and carried him to the window.

'The chief might have a point,' he said as they looked to the street below. 'See here, miss, Ross and Eileen Hunter were leading separate lives, okay? So, what if she was planning to fleece him anyway and his death was just an unfortunate coincidence?'

Munro took a bite of a bacon roll, brushed the crumbs from his shirt, and pondered the possibility.

'It's a feasible enough scenario,' he said. 'However, the only way she'd be able to access his investments whilst he was alive, would be to do it fraudulently, forging his signature and the like, and that wouldnae be easy if they were living together.'

'I'm getting a headache,' said West. 'Dougal, what about Ross Hunter? Did you find anything on his computer?'

'Oh aye,' said Dougal. 'Plenty. About four weeks ago he sent the same email to all four of his pension providers requesting the necessary forms to draw-down his funds as a cash lump sum.'

'That could be to finance the purchase of their villa in Mallorca,' said Munro, 'although, bearing in mind the length of time it takes to complete such transactions, I'd say he'd left it a wee bit late, so perhaps that's not the reason after all. Have they released the funds?'

'Well, nothing's showing on his account,' said Dougal. 'The fact of the matter is, he may not have even returned the forms yet.'

West, intent on hammering a square peg into a round hole, raised her right arm and clicked her fingers excitedly.

'Hold up!' she said. 'What about Eileen Hunter? Maybe she sent those emails!'

'It's possible,' said Dougal. 'If she had the password to his computer, and his email account.'

'No, no,' said Duncan, 'that's not likely, not by any stretch of the imagination.'

'Why not?'

'Look, if they were a loved-up couple then, aye, maybe, but not in their situation. No, no, Ross Hunter would've had everything under lock and key, trust me.'

'There's something else,' said Dougal. 'I found an email from a firm of solicitors on Wellington Square. Now, the intriguing thing about this is that there was obviously some kind of an email conversation going on between them but they've all been deleted, bar the last one, and that says "Dear Mr Hunter, blah, blah, blah, further to our previous correspondence all we require now is your signature, we look forward to seeing you at 2pm," etcetera, etcetera, etcetera.'

'Maybe that's to do with the villa, as well,' said West. 'Chase it up, would you? Find out exactly what it is he was meant to be signing.'

'No bother.'

'Right, me and Jimbo are taking Murdo for a walk.'

'Are you joking?' said Duncan. 'No offence, miss, but you've not got time for doggy duties. We've enough on our plates as it is.'

'As I was saying, me and Jimbo are taking Murdo for a walk... to the recycling centre. We're going to see Peggy McClure again.'

'How so? She'll be getting sick of the sight of you.'

'Remember all those times Ross Hunter went to visit his son at the boarding school? Well, he wasn't alone, McClure was keeping him company.'

'That,' said Duncan, 'is what some teachers refer to as an extra-curricular activity. I wonder if his wife knew.'

'Well, we'll soon find out. Right, we'll leave you to it.'

'Hold on,' said Dougal, 'I'm not done yet.'

'Come on then, make it snappy.'

'Two things. Forensics, and The Bear.'

'DCI Elliot? What's he want?'

'He says you're not to leave the building until you've seen him. He's some news for you and he says he's to tell you face to face.'

'That sounds a bit ominous.'

'I think it is. You should have seen the look on his face last night, pure raging, he was.'

'In that case,' said West, 'I'd better pop along the corridor now and get it out of the way. Wish me luck, and if you get a chance, see if you can find some empty cardboard boxes.'

'What for?'

'All your stuff. We might have to clear our desks in a bit.'

* * *

Suspecting he may have underestimated Dougal's ability to confront adversity with the resolve of William Wallace at an independence rally, Munro, tossing the dog a toasted crust, smiled sympathetically as the young detective stared, nonplussed, into space.

'Well, I'll say this for Charlie, she certainly knows how to bolster a team's spirits, I'll give her that.'

'Aye, you're not wrong there,' said Duncan. 'What's the betting she comes back in a black cloak with a scythe over her shoulder.'

'That's fair taken the wind out my sails,' said Dougal. 'I wasn't expecting that.'

'Well, as I'm far as I'm concerned, it's not over till the DCI sings; in the meantime, we've still got a job to do so, come on, pal, what's all this about forensics?'

'Oh, aye, forensics! You'll like this, it's good news. They've retrieved two separate strands of DNA from the bed linen, one from a blood stain and the other from a semen deposit.'

'Result! Hold on, if it's good news, why are you not smiling?'

'There's no match,' said Dougal. 'For either.'

'Well, that's just smashing,' said Duncan. 'It's like having the keys to a Jag, and no Jag.'

'Come, come,' said Munro, 'if everything was that easy, you'd be out of a job.'

'No offence, chief, but I think you're tempting fate. Okay, think about it, if there's no match, then at least it proves Navinder Singh-Gill wasn't involved after all – he was telling the truth. And if there was blood on the sheets, then I'm guessing that has to belong to Meena, so I need to get her in for a swab.'

'Good luck with that,' said Dougal. 'She's not agreed so far.'

'Well, if she still refuses, I'll just have to pay her a visit and borrow something of hers, like a hairbrush, maybe.'

'I'd watch yourself if I were you,' said Munro, 'there are rules about that kind of thing.'

'Off the record, chief, you know what I think about rules. So, I'll give her a wee bell, then I'll take myself off to the pub; with any luck I'll bump into those two neds who showed up at her house.'

* * *

Whilst struggling to cope with the pressures of fulfilling her duties as a junior officer in London's Square Mile, a situation made worse by the unreasonable demands of her misogynistic colleagues and further exacerbated by the emotional turmoil of a broken engagement to a philandering fiancée, West – who'd taken to alleviating the stress by crawling into bed with Count Smirnoff and taking more sick leave than a hypochondriac with an immune deficiency – had, with a raft of reprimands under her belt, become blasé about receiving bad news.

However, as a harbinger of doom, the task of conveying the uncertainty of the department's future to the lesser ranks made her feel distinctly uncomfortable.

She stood in the doorway with her hands in her back pockets and mustered a tight-lipped smile.

'Jeez-oh,' said Dougal. 'So that it's then. How long have we got?'

'End of day,' said West. 'You'd better get those boxes.'

'Right, that's me away,' said Duncan. 'I need to go pack a fleece and my walking boots.'

Munro, unfazed by the inevitable gloom, awarded himself a knowing smile as the imposing bulk of DCI Elliot loomed behind West.

'Dear God,' he said, 'I've stumbled across a wake. Have you not heard the news? There's no need to rush, just make sure you've cleared your desks by five, okay?'

'Okay?' said Duncan. 'Is that it, then?'

'Is what, it?'

'Is that all you have to say? After all this time? We're being put out to pasture and you've not even a word of apology?'

'What are you havering about?' said Elliot. 'We're getting a refurb', that's all. Brand new kit for all of us. They'll be wiring us up overnight, that's why you have to clear your desks.'

'So, we're not being given the heave-ho?'

'No-one's going anywhere, especially you, DS Reid, and you've James to thank for that! It was him who made them see sense. It was him who told them, quite categorically I might add, that two sergeants were better than none.'

'That's cracking news,' said Duncan reaching for his phone, 'apologies for, you know. Sorry, I've a wee text, here.'

'If it's the recruitment agency, tell them you're sorted.'

'Oh, you dancer! It's Meena Singh-Gill. Thanks to her brother, she's agreed to a swab. I'll fetch her now.'

'Well, things are looking up,' said West. 'Dougal, you start packing. Jimbo, Murdo. Heel.'

Chapter 22

Suppressing her ire at riding shotgun in an antiquated Peugeot while her Defender sat idle in the car park, West, who'd sailed through her driving test with an impressive display of roadcraft behind the wheel of her father's leviathan of a Land Cruiser at the tender age of seventeen, sighed with frustration as Munro pootled past the industrial estate with all the zip of a hearse on its way to the cemetery.

'Is this some kind of a record?' she said as she lowered the visor against the glare of the sun.

'If you're referring to our velocity,' said Munro, 'then unlike yourself, Charlie, I prefer to keep within the designated speed limits.'

'Actually, I was referring to the weather. It's getting toasty again.'

'This is Caledonia, lassie, not the arctic circle. You'll be reaching for the sunscreen by four o'clock, trust me.'

* * *

Leafing through a well-worn copy of *Country Life* that she'd pillaged from a box full of discarded magazines, Peggy McClure, lounging on the bench with a mug of coffee by her side, grinned as Munro, in his short-sleeved shirt and polarised sunglasses, approached with Murdo tugging at the lead.

'Oh, Mr Munro!' she said as she stooped to pat the dog. 'Fancy seeing you. Who's this beauty?'

'He goes by the name of Murdo,' said Munro. 'He's a rescue.'

'Away! Why would anyone want to get rid of this fella?'

'A change of personal circumstances, so I'm told.'

'Well, he's landed with his bum in the butter, I can see that. How old is he?'

'We're of a similar age,' said Munro, 'although I have to say, he's ageing somewhat better than myself.'

'So, what brings you here?'

'I do,' said West, as she wandered towards them. 'You're not busy, are you?'

'No, no. There's not much happening just now so I thought I'd have myself a wee break.'

'Good. So you've got time for a chat, then?'

'Aye, no bother,' said McClure. 'Have a seat.'

'No, ta. I'll let these two have it, they need it more than me.'

'So, how can I help, Inspector? To be honest, I wasn't expecting to see you again.'

'That makes two of us,' said West, 'but we need to talk about your mate, Hunter.'

'Ross?'

'Yep.'

'Dear, dear,' said McClure, shaking her head, 'it's pure tragic what happened to him. So young, too. Have they planted him yet?'

'No. That won't happen for a while yet, at least, not until we've finished our investigation.'

'Perhaps you'll let me know when that is. The man deserves to have at least one mourner at his funeral.'

'What do you mean?'

'Well, with his wife away, and his son…'

'Hold up,' said West. 'Who said anything about his wife being away?'

McClure's eyes flashed between West and Munro.

'Did you not tell me?' she said. 'The last time you came?'

'Nope.'

'Oh, well, I don't know where I got that from, then.'

'Well, I'd try and remember if I were you, because I'll need an answer before we go. Right, about Ross.'

'What about him?'

'You said you'd not seen him for months and months, a year, maybe. Is that right, or am I losing my marbles?'

'No, no, you're perfectly right.'

'Good. And the time before that?'

'Oh, now you're asking,' said McClure, her face crinkling as she frowned. 'Probably a good month or two, I'd say.'

'But despite the fact you'd not seen each other, you still remember him quite, what's the word, *vividly*, don't you? I mean, the way you described him: kind, caring, good-looking. I'm guessing you must have really fancied him.'

'Aye, well, I've made no bones about that, Inspector. It's like I told you before, if I could have nabbed him for myself, I would have done.'

West, pausing for effect under the guise of pondering her next question, slipped her hands into her pockets and toed the gravel beneath her feet.

'What about Kieran?' she said, glancing up at the clear, blue sky. 'Do you miss him too?'

'Aye, he's a wee darling, that boy.'

'His old man was soft on him, wasn't he? He loved him to bits.'

'Right enough, he missed him like mad. He'd drive all the way to Lathallan every weekend. Come hell or high water, he'd be there.'

'That's dedication for you,' said West, 'but one thing I don't get is, how do you know he went every weekend if you hadn't seen him?'

McClure leaned back on the bench and shielded her eyes with a hand across her forehead.

'He told me,' she said, squinting at West. 'Well, texted me. Every now and then I'd get a wee text. Nothing exciting, just an update on how he was doing.'

'That was nice of him, considering the state of your relationship.'

'Well, that's just the kind of fella he was.'

'What about Kieran?' said West. 'It seems you two had quite a bond. Do you ever hear from him?'

'No, I'm afraid not.'

'Do you think he misses you like you miss him?'

'I'd like to think so. Maybe.'

West took a step forward, stared blankly at the ground, and twisted her foot as if stubbing out a cigarette.

'You know what?' she said, lowering her voice. 'I'm no mother, but in my experience most kids have minds like sieves, they have a habit of forgetting things all too quickly, so if you haven't seen him in over a year then I'd have to say that as far as he is concerned, you're probably ancient history.'

'That's charming, that.'

'But here's the thing,' said West, 'I don't think it has been a year. I think Kieran remembers you like it was yesterday. Or last week to be precise.'

'Sorry,' said McClure, 'I'm not with you, I'm getting confused.'

'The charade's over,' said West. 'You see, Miss McClure, I know for a fact that you saw Ross Hunter last weekend. I know for a fact that you saw his son last weekend. And I know for fact that you've been with Ross Hunter every weekend for the last year or so.'

'Don't be daft.'

'And I know… because Kieran told me.'

McClure glanced at Munro and lowered her head.

'I see,' she said. 'Well, that's another skeleton out of the closet.'

'Why didn't you tell us that before?'

'I didn't think it was important.'

West slowly inched her way towards McClure until she was close enough to cast her in shadow, leaned forward, and glowered.

'There's a big difference,' she said, softly, 'between not telling us something because you didn't think it was important enough, and blatant lying.'

'Okay, my mistake,' said McClure, raising her hands, 'I shouldn't have lied. So, what are you going to do? Charge me for withholding information or something?'

'You're lucky we're not in court,' said West, 'because everything you've told us from day one of this investigation is tantamount to perjury. Wasting police time. That's six months in the pokey. So, what exactly was your relationship with Ross Hunter?'

McClure smiled at the dog and sighed.

'It was close,' she said.

'How close? Close enough for him to buy you that ring?'

'Aye. We had plans.'

'You had plans?' said West, mockingly. 'Sorry Miss McClure, but why do I get the impression that your plans and his were not entirely the same?'

'What do you mean?'

'A few days ago, when I told you that he'd died, you reacted like your neighbour's cat had been run over. It wasn't the kind of reaction I'd expect from someone who'd just been told that the person they were madly in love with had been bludgeoned to death.'

'I'm not the emotional type,' said McClure. 'Besides, love's too strong a word for what we had.'

'And what word would you use?'

'Need,' said McClure. 'We had a need for each other. Is that a crime these days too?'

'As good as,' said West, looking over her shoulder, 'especially in this instance. Can I help?'

There were, as listed in any thesaurus, several polite words that could be used to describe Gordon Miller, ranging from curious and inquisitive, to quizzical and inquiring, but for West the most appropriate were undoubtedly interfering, meddlesome, and downright nosey.

Ditching his shirt in favour of a hi-vis vest, he strode – armed with a smile, a broom, and an empty bin bag – directly towards them, stopping abruptly as Murdo, dropping his tail, began barking incessantly.

'He's a wee gob on him,' said Miller. 'What's his problem?'

'Did you know, there's a wee saying,' said Munro, 'if your dog doesnae like someone, then you shouldnae either.'

'How so?'

'Call it instinct. It's the one thing we two have in common, apart from a dislike of vegetables, that is. Now, what do you want?'

'I just thought I'd see if I could help.'

'And what makes you think you can help?' said West.

'Oh, you know, I just…'

'Do you know a bloke called Ross Hunter?'

'Hunter? No, doesn't ring any bells.'

'Then you can't help. Now, if you don't mind.'

'No, you're alright,' said Miller, 'I'm in no hurry. I'll just sit a while and…'

'Are you deaf?' said Munro. 'See here, sonny, this is a private conversation. Now, on you go before I do you for interfering with a police investigation.'

Miller curled his lip as he caught his reflection in Munro's tinted, blue shades.

'Right,' he said, gritting his teeth, 'that's me told. Peggy, you know where I'll be.'

West nodded at Miller as he walked away.

'What is it with him?' she said. 'Every time we meet, he turns up like a bad penny.'

'Oh, it's just his way,' said McClure.

'You mean he's paranoid?'

'No, protective, I suppose. Clingy.'

'And is he clingy with other women, or just you?'

'I wouldn't know,' said McClure, 'I've not seen him with other women.'

Munro removed his glasses, crossed his legs, and smiled as he turned to face McClure.

'How long have you two known each other?' he said.

'He was here when I joined.'

'You appear to have quite a rapport. You obviously get along.'

'Aye, we're pals. Good pals.'

West looked down at McClure, folded her arms, and raised one eyebrow.

'I'm not in the habit of repeating myself,' she said, 'but in this case I'll make an exception. Misleading an investigation. Wasting police time.'

McClure, fearing her reputation was on the line, rubbed her thighs with the palms of her hands, stared back at West, and sighed.

'Look, I'm not a slapper, okay? It was a long time ago.'

'What was?'

'Gordy and me. A one-off. That's all it was. I'd given up teaching, my head was mince; he was young, not bad looking, so I thought, why not?'

'Why not indeed. But?'

'But he'll not let it go. He's got it into his head that one day I'm going to give in and rekindle our romance.'

'Romance?'

'His word, not mine. Frankly, I think he's just keen to get his leg over again.'

'Is he hounding you?' said Munro. 'Pestering you? Intimidating you? Hanging around when he should be in his bed?'

'No, no. Nothing like that.'

'You're sure?'

'Aye. He's just a wee bit insecure, is all.'

Munro, sensing that McClure's defence of Miller was based on fear rather than compassion, smiled sympathetically.

'Tell me, Miss McClure,' he said, 'is Mr Miller aware of your involvement with Ross Hunter? Your personal history, as it were?'

'He told you himself, he's not heard of him.'

'With all due respect,' said Munro, 'I'm not interested in what he said, I'm asking you.'

'Well, the answer's no. He knows nothing about him.'

'Would you say he's the jealous type?'

'Who? Gordy?'

'Aye, he seems a wee bit... jumpy. Possessive, even. That's the kind of behaviour I'd expect from someone who'd fallen foul of the green-eyed monster.'

'I wouldn't know.'

'So, hypothetically speaking,' said Munro, 'if you were to become involved with somebody else, you dinnae think he'd be upset?'

'Why should he?' said McClure. 'Let's face it, he's young, Mr Munro. He has plenty of time to find himself a girl. God knows why he's chasing an oldie like me, I've more wrinkles than a prune past its sell-by.'

West, unimpressed by McClure's self-deprecating sense of humour, stood with her hands on her hips and gazed at her impassively.

'Right, well, that's all been very informative,' she said. 'Now all we need to do is get everything you've just told us down as a formal statement.'

'Why?'

'Let's just say, that way, we can rule you out of the equation. So, you've got a choice. You can either come with us voluntarily and we'll get it stitched in an hour or so, or if you refuse, I can arrest you now on suspicion of attempting to pervert the course of justice. But before you decide, a word to the wise. If I have to caution you, you won't be going home for at least twenty-four hours. I'll see to that personally.'

'Well, if put it like that,' said McClure, 'I'll come voluntarily, then.'

'Good. You've got two minutes to grab your coat.'

'Coat? You mean now?'

'That's exactly what I mean.'

'But what about work?' said McClure. 'And Bobby the Bruce?'

'Go make your excuses,' said Munro. 'We'll stop by the house and collect Bobby, he can keep Murdo company until you've signed on the dotted line.'

West took a seat on the bench, picked up Murdo, and placed him on her lap while they waited for McClure to return.

'You do know that under section 57 of the Highway Code, if this mutt is travelling in the car, he should be restrained in the back seat?'

'That's an advisory clause,' said Munro as he pulled on his shades, 'it's not in legislation.'

'So, you're going to let him travel up front with you?'

'Of course, Charlie. He's like yourself, until he gets used to travelling alone, he'll need all the reassurance he can get.'

'Well, if that's true,' said West, 'he'll always be in the front. Do you know what's really annoying about your blooming sunglasses?'

'Don't tell me, they make me look like a young Tony Curtis.'

'Who?'

'Doesnae matter.'

'Well, it's the fact that I can't see your eyes. I can't see what you're thinking.'

'I'm thinking,' said Munro, 'that there's something rum about that Miller chap.'

'Well, that's what I've been trying to tell you all along but you wouldn't listen.'

'No, Charlie, you've been sharing your suspicion that there was something going on between McClure and Miller, and you were right. However, I am talking about the man himself.'

'Come on, then,' said West. 'Why?'

'Intuition,' said Munro, 'based on his obvious paranoia and his propensity for sticking his nose into other folk's business. I'll run a check on him while you're dealing with McClure.'

Chapter 23

Intent on avoiding the congestion of the town centre, Munro – opting for the scenic route – cruised along the promenade with the sun glinting off the Firth and toyed with the notion of continuing on to the esplanade where Murdo could frolic in the surf whilst he indulged in a raspberry ripple but, with McClure seething silently in the rear view mirror, and West on the verge of nodding off, he reluctantly returned to the stagnant atmosphere of the office instead.

'You're looking awful red, miss,' said Dougal, as West shuffled through the door. 'Do you not have any sunscreen?'

'To be fair, Dougal, that's a bit like asking Lawrence of Arabia if he'd packed his wellies. How was I to know I'd need flipping sunscreen up here?'

Duncan swung his feet onto the desk and laughed.

'You know your trouble, miss?' he said. 'You're pure gullible, everything you've heard about the weather is a fallacy, apart from the midges, that is. It's not as hot as London, I'll give you that, but it's hot enough. Where's the chief?'

'Bringing up the rear,' said West. 'He's setting up a crèche.'

Dougal backed his chair to the wall as two panting terriers, their size belying their strength, dragged Munro into the office.

'Are you starting a puppy farm?' he said. 'Because if you are, I'm of a mind to tell The Bear I'd be happy with a transfer after all.'

'Haud your wheesht!' said Munro as he fetched a water bowl for the dogs. 'This one belongs to McClure, he'll be on his way soon enough.'

'And how was she?' said Duncan. 'Peggy McClure?'

'Like butter wouldn't melt,' said West, 'until I threatened to do her for impersonating Pinocchio, then she soon bucked her ideas up.'

'Sorry?'

'She came clean about her and Ross Hunter, they've been at it for donkey's years. Right, I'm having a quick brew before I take her statement. Anyone else?'

'Aye, the usual,' said Munro, 'milk and three. Dougal, this Gordon Miller fellow, I need to find out everything I can about the chap, perhaps you'd care to help me out. If you can spare the time, that is.'

'Aye, no bother, but you'll have to give me an hour, boss. I'm dealing with Hunter's solicitor just now.'

'I'll give you a hand,' said Duncan. 'I'm not busy.'

'So, you've sorted Meena Singh-Gill?' said West. 'Has she been and gone?'

'Aye, all swabbed and sampled, miss. We just have to wait for her to show on the system, then hopefully we can eliminate one of the stains on the bed sheets as hers.'

'Good. And next?'

'I'll be away down the pub in an hour or so. I'm going to see if I can find those two delinquents.'

'A bit early for the boozer, isn't it?'

'No, no. They finish early on a Friday,' said Duncan, 'and frankly, I'd rather catch them before they've had a skinful.'

'Quite right,' said Munro. 'Two against one doesnae stack the odds in your favour. Just you watch yourself.'

'No danger, chief. I'll not take any chances, trust me. So, Gordon Miller, what's he done?'

'Maybe nothing,' said Munro, 'we'll not know until we have a look.'

'Right,' said West as she drained her mug, 'I'd better go and deal with McClure, you lot behave yourselves.'

* * *

As a retired officer who'd once regarded the fax machine, the cassette tape, and the VHS recorder as 'cutting-edge', Munro, blaming developments in the world of digital communication for spawning a generation of narcissistic nincompoops incapable of memorising telephone numbers or reading maps, remained wary of utilising the technology himself.

Duncan watched from across the desk as he delicately stabbed the keyboard like a short-sighted stenographer, verifying each character of Miller's name as it appeared on the screen, before calling his laboured progress to a halt.

'It's not looking good, chief,' he said. 'There's only one Gordon Miller on the electoral register, and it's not him.'

'How on earth can that be?'

'Sorry, chief, it's not my fault, but it's not him.'

'No, no,' said Munro, 'what I mean is, how the devil did you do that so quickly?'

'Oh, it's just habit, I suppose. I can type as fast as you can think.'

'I'm glad to hear it,' said Munro. 'If it was the other way round, you'd be in trouble.'

'Aye, there's nothing here on social media either,' said Dougal.

'I thought you were dealing with Ross Hunter's solicitor?'

'I am, boss, but I've two hands, and two computers.'

'Dear God,' said Munro, 'if there's one way of showing your age, it's trying to keep up with the likes of you.'

'Not so,' said Duncan, reassuringly. 'See here, chief, without these at our disposal, we'd be crap, whereas you don't need an algorithm to help you solve a crime.'

'Flattered, I'm sure. So, there's no sign of this Miller chap anywhere, you say?'

'Not yet.'

'Then start at the beginning. Contact the council and get a list of all the employees at the recycling centre, let's see if he's on there.'

'Roger that.'

* * *

Dougal, who preferred to graze on small portions of high-energy foods to maintain a constant level of alertness rather than binge on a calorie-laden lunch and have to fight the ensuing desire to grab forty winks on the couch afterwards, cleared an empty packet of pistachios from his desk and checked his watch.

'I'm peckish,' he said, 'and I've not moved from my seat all day. Are you not hungry?'

'We are,' said Munro, 'but we'd best wait for Charlie. They always give us a discount at the café when we buy in bulk.'

'This,' said Duncan, 'is getting murkier the deeper we dig.'

'How so?' said Munro.

'There's no-one by the name of Miller on the council list of employees, but there is a fella called Gordon. Gordon Dickie.'

'Ho-ho!' said Dougal with a snicker. 'I bet he got ribbed for that as a wean!'

'Do you have a photograph?'

'I do,' said Duncan, as he flipped the laptop to face Munro. 'Is that him?'

'Aye, that's him, right enough. Okay, let's go again, only this time we're looking for anything we can find on Gordon Dickie.'

'We?'

'By which, of course, I mean you. I shall provide logistical support by making a round of tea. Oh, and one of you get on to national records, see if he's changed his name, either by deed poll or statutory declaration.'

Before Munro had made it to the kitchenette, let alone managed to fill the kettle, Dougal, his fingers flying across the keyboard with the dexterity of a virtuoso performer rattling off a rendition of *The Flight of the Bumblebee*, had already cleared the first hurdle with Duncan coming in a close second.

'He's not on the national computer, boss,' he said, 'which means he's not got a record.'

'But he is on the council register,' said Duncan. 'Paterson Street. There's two other folk listed at the same address, family by the looks of it.'

'Hold on,' said Dougal, his eyes darting about the screen, 'Paterson Street, that sounds familiar. Jeez-oh, that's the address for one of the Aygos. That's where the two pensioners live.'

'Did uniform not call on them?' said Munro. 'When they were checking on those vehicles?'

'They did, aye.'

'Then why did they not say Miller was living under the same roof?'

'I've no idea, boss, maybe…'

Dougal's words tailed off as Duncan leapt from his seat and stood behind him.

'Let's see that photo from the camera at the jewellers,' he said. 'Chief, get yourself here a minute. Look at that, do you think that's him? Do you think that's Miller?'

Munro pulled his spectacles from his breast pocket, leaned into the screen, and squinted.

'Och, I cannae tell from that angle,' he said, 'it's just the top of his head. Do you not have any other images? Any of his face?'

'No,' said Dougal, 'that's the best we have.'

'We should bring him in,' said Duncan, 'after all, Westy said he's got a temper and a half.'

'Calm your jets,' said Munro. 'He does have a temper, aye. Well, actually, it's more of an *attitude*, but before we do anything, we need to establish whether he actually lives at that address. Then we have to see if he has access to the Aygo. If the answer is yes on both counts, then we have grounds to bring him in.'

'Will that not slow things down?'

'As they say in the carpentry trade, laddie: measure twice, cut once. Okay?'

* * *

West, looking happier than she had an hour earlier, breezed through the door and grinned.

'You're looking pleased with yourself, Charlie,' said Munro. 'Has McClure had an accident?'

'I wish. There's something about that woman that brings out the best in me.'

'You're referring, of course, to the vindictive side of your nature.'

'I don't have a vindictive side,' said West. 'I'm just not keen on liars, that's all.'

'So,' said Duncan, 'is that you done?'

'Yup, I've just got to give this mutt back to McClure, then she can be on her way. What have you lot been up to?'

'Gordon Miller,' said Duncan. 'He's not Gordon Miller, at all. He's Gordon Dickie.'

'Poor bloke. That's not a name you'd forget in a hurry.'

'We're working on him now, and guess what? He's living at the same address as one of those Aygos.'

'Which means,' said Munro, 'that you and I, Charlie, have a wee house call to make.'

'You're not seriously suggesting that he was the one who clobbered Ross Hunter over the head?'

'I'm suggesting nothing of the sort. I'm simply suggesting that we pay him a visit.'

'Okay, if we must,' said West, 'but first I need to get rid of this dog and then, I need to eat.'

'I'll nip to the café,' said Dougal. 'Who's for what?'

'Nothing for me,' said Duncan. 'I'm away to the pub.'

'I'm not fussed,' said Munro. 'Something simple. A square sausage will do me. Crisp mind, I'll not take it if it's undercooked. And I'd like a white roll with butter, not margarine. And don't forget the sauce. Brown. Not too much.'

'Miss?'

'The same,' said West, 'but make it two.'

Chapter 24

Whilst most of the residents of Whitletts and Dalmilling were of the belief that their semi-suburban existence on the outskirts of town was undeniably enhanced by the presence of a sprawling retail park, an activity centre, and a bowling club, those averse to shopping and sports who craved nothing more than a quiet pint within staggering distance of their homes, found their choice of pubs limited to two, with the Redstone Inn – an earthy boozer without a television, a karaoke machine, or even a jukebox – proving the most popular.

Duncan, deeming his heavy, leather car coat far too restrictive should he have to scuffle with his prey, left it on the back seat of the car, pushed his phone deep into his trouser pocket, and pulled his tee shirt down over his waist to hide the cuffs clipped to his belt.

The bar, already heaving with shift workers, pensioners, and dole merchants intent on getting the weekend off to a blistering start, reverberated with the sound of biased predictions for Saturday's big match, the dire state of the government, and clandestine offers of cut-price cigarettes which had conveniently fallen off the back of a lorry.

'Orange juice, please, hen,' he said, waving a fiver at the barmaid.

'Are you wanting a shot in that?'

'Not for me, thanks. I'm driving.'

Feigning the arrival of a message, Duncan pulled his phone from his pocket and surreptitiously scanned the pub for two gentlemen who, according to Ash, would resemble Abbott and Costello in a couple of hard hats, and froze as he caught sight of a lithe, bottle-blonde sitting at a corner table.

'Crap,' he mumbled under his breath as she beckoned him over.

'I never thought I'd see you in my local,' said McClure coyly, 'what brings you to this neck of the woods?'

'Oh, just a wee bit of business,' said Duncan.

'Official?'

'No, no. That's me until Monday.'

'So, you're starting the weekend with the rest of us?'

'Too early for me,' said Duncan. 'And yourself? Are you okay?'

'I'm getting there,' said McClure, rolling her eyes. 'You'll not believe the morning I've had.'

'How so?'

'I've been cooped up with your boss and that Mr Munro, they seem to think…'

'That's plenty,' said Duncan, raising his hand, 'no offence, but I'm off duty. I'm sure they'll tell me what they've been up to, if they think I need to know.'

'Fair enough,' said McClure. 'So, I'm wondering…'

'Aye?'

'I'm wondering what kind of business you could be doing in a pub like this when you're not a regular.'

'As it happens,' said Duncan, 'I'm looking for a fella.'

'It's not that kind of a pub.'

'I'll start again. I'm flogging my motor, see, and the fella who wants it told me to meet him here.'

'Well, I know all the locals,' said McClure. 'What's his name?'

'Nav. Indian fella.'

'Oh, I know Nav; not to speak to, mind, but he's here most weekends. Always on the make.'

'Sorry?'

'Wheeling and dealing, if you know what I mean.'

'Too much information,' said Duncan. 'I'm here to meet the fella, not arrest him.'

Duncan stepped to one side as a surly individual with a face like a bulldog chewing a wasp brushed past, placed two pints of lager on the table, and sat down.

'I'll give you some peace,' said Duncan. 'I never realised you had company.'

'Nonsense,' said McClure. 'You stay as long as you like. This is Gordon. Gordy, this is…'

'Alright, pal?' said Duncan, cutting her short. 'So, you work with Peggy, is that right?'

'Aye, what of it?' said Miller. 'Have you got a problem with that?'

'I don't think it's me with the problem,' said Duncan as he drained his glass. 'I should go.'

'He's waiting on Nav,' said McClure. 'He's after buying his car.'

'Nav, buying a motor?' said Miller, jokingly. 'Good luck with that, pal. He doesn't drive.'

'Well, maybe he's after it for someone who does. Look, I can't hang around, I'll have to give him a call later.'

'Oh, hold on, Sergeant,' said McClure. 'Gordy knows where he lives, he can give you the address.'

Miller took a sip of lager and glanced up at Duncan.

'Sergeant?' he said.

'Aye, that's right,' said McClure. 'Sergeant Reid, he's been involved with the hoo-ha at work.'

'Excuse me,' said Miller. 'I need a fag.'

Duncan waited for Miller to leave, turned to McClure, and smiled.

'Something I said?'

'It's not your fault,' said McClure, 'he has a thing about the police.'

'Oh, aye? Something to hide, has he?'

'Just a persecution complex.'

McClure waved and cooed as another familiar figure, desperate to quench his thirst, barged through the door.

'Alright, Tommy?' she said. 'Did you not see Gordy?'

'No. Where?'

'Outside. He just popped out for a smoke.'

'Well, he's not there now,' said Tommy. 'You okay for a drink, hen?'

Duncan glanced around the pub, watching as McClure's friend, a short, rotund gent with an ample belly and a head like a polished bowling ball, made his way to the bar.

'That's Tommy,' said McClure. 'Tommy Fraser. He handles all the heavy stuff, you know, wardrobes, and freezers, and the like. Lovely fella, he is. Ever so polite.'

'Oh, so he works with you, too?'

'Aye, he's more a pal of Gordy's than mine. Thick as thieves, the pair of them.'

'Right, that's me away,' said Duncan. 'Do me a favour, Miss McClure, if you see Nav, tell him to give me a call, okay?'

'No bother, Sergeant. You take yourself off and have a good weekend.'

Duncan glanced up and down the street, took a swift look around the rear of the pub and, with no sign of Miller, called the office as he made his way back to the car.

* * *

Unlike some of the pebble-dashed semis on Paterson Street which, after years of neglect, were in need of a good lick of paint and a gallon or two of weed killer, one in particular, incongruous by its appearance, appeared to be owned by budding horticulturalists who epitomised the definition of 'house-proud'.

Munro nodded approvingly at the neatly-trimmed hedge and vast array of potted plants blooming by the front door as he stepped from the Defender and gently dabbed the beads of perspiration peppering his forehead.

'You alright, Jimbo?' said West as she lifted Murdo from the passenger seat. 'Not too warm for you, is it?'

'No, no, I was simply roasting behind the windscreen, that's all.'

'Well, imagine how this mutt felt.'

'At least he could get his head out the window.'

'Even so, just say if you're feeling ropey, I can do this, if you like.'

'Nonsense,' said Munro. 'I told you, Charlie, I'm perfectly fine.'

'Okay, in that case, you can do the honours. They'll like you more than they'll like me.'

'And how on earth do you figure that?'

'Well, you know, age and stuff. They're pensioners. They'll probably open up to an old duffer like you.'

* * *

A diminutive lady dressed in navy-blue slacks and a pale, lambswool cardigan who obviously took as much pride in her appearance as she did with her garden, opened the door and beamed at Munro as though visitors were a rarity.

'Hello, there,' she said warmly. 'Can I help?'

'Mrs Dickie?'

'Aye.'

'James Munro. And this is Detective Inspector West.'

'And the doggie,' said Dickie, 'is he a detective too?'

'More of mascot, really,' said West. 'Would you mind if we had a quick word?'

'Not at all, come away through, but I'm afraid you'll have to leave the doggie here.'

'No, you're alright,' said Munro. 'We'll not keep you long. It's about your motor car.'

'Oh, we had the police round the other night asking about that.'

'I know,' said Munro, smiling as his steely-blue eyes glinted in the sun. 'That's why we're here. You see, we understand the officer who knocked your door showed you a wee photograph of a chap they were trying to trace, and apparently you told them that nobody lived here but yourselves, is that correct?'

'It is, aye,' said Dickie, looking embarrassed, 'but to be honest, I didn't have my glasses on and we were having our supper, so I wanted rid of him as quick as possible. Did I do something wrong?'

'No, no, but perhaps we can start again.'

'Will I need my specs?'

'No. You see, Mrs Dickie, we believe the gentleman we'd like to speak to goes by the name of Gordon Miller, but there's no-one of that name registered at this address.'

'No, there wouldn't be,' said Dickie. 'It's my son you're talking about. Is he in some kind of bother?'

'Nah, nothing serious,' said West. 'We just reckon he might be able to help us out, that's all.'

'I see.'

'But he lives here, does he? Your son?'

'Aye, he does indeed.'

'So, about the name,' said Munro, 'why does he use "Miller"?'

'Miller's my maiden name,' said Dickie. 'He's used it ever since he left school.'

'And why would he do that?'

'Because of the torment he suffered. Oh, I know it sounds funny now but you'd not believe the abuse he got.'

'Abuse?'

'From the kids, relentless they were, with their constant jibes, day in, day out. It was Dickie Head, Stinky Dickie, Wee Dickie.'

'So he was bullied?' said West.

'In a way, aye, I suppose it was bullying, but Gordon's always been a big lad, he didn't take it lying down.'

'Oh?'

'No,' said Dickie. 'He battered every last boy that dared to take the mick. Unfortunately, that earned him the nickname Detention Dickie. He couldn't win.'

'So, when did he start using your name?'

'As I say, as soon as he left school and took his first job.'

'So, it's not an official thing?' said Munro. 'I mean, he's not changed his name by deed poll or anything like that?'

'No, no. All his pals know him as Miller, the only folk who know his real name, apart from ourselves, would be his employers.'

'And they were?'

'The butcher on Main Street, and the council.'

'And that's it?' said West. 'He's not had any other jobs?'

'None.'

'So, tell me, Mrs Dickie, your son, Gordon, does he have access to your vehicle? The Aygo?'

'He does, but he rarely uses it; only if his is in the garage for a wee service or something.'

'And is it? In the garage?'

'Aye! It is. MOT, I think, but they're wanting a hundred and twenty pounds for tyres and he's not got the cash. Not until pay day.'

'Does he have keys to your car?'

'No, we've only the two,' said Dickie. 'One for myself, and one for my husband.'

'And is it here, now?' said West.

'Aye, it's in the garage.'

'Can we take a look?'

'Of course, help yourself; it's not locked.'

Munro, fearing the old lady would sustain a back injury if she attempted to lift the door, heaved open the up-and-over, stood back, and turned to face her.

'Well, that's not right,' she said. 'It was here this morning.'

'Do you think your son could have borrowed it?'

'Well, I suppose, but it's Friday, he's usually at the pub. I'll check with my husband, just hold on a tick.'

West, grinning with excitement, thumped Munro playfully on the shoulder as Dickie disappeared into the house.

'You know what this means?' she said, in a strained whisper. 'It means Miller might be the one who walloped Hunter after all.'

'Well, it's certainly looking that way, Charlie,' said Munro as he pulled Murdo to the shade of the garage, 'but the question is, why? Why would Miller want to attack Ross Hunter?'

'Oh, we'll figure that one out later,' said West, 'what we need to do right now is bring him in so we can verify it's him on the CCTV.'

'Panic over!' said Dickie, waving her arms as she ambled up the drive. 'Gordon came by not half an hour ago, whipped the key from the peg, and was off again. I must have been out the back.'

'Have you any idea where he might have gone?' said Munro. 'Did he have appointments to keep? Friends to see?'

'Not that I'm aware of. I can only assume he's away to the garage on Somerset Road, I really can't think where else he would go.'

* * *

Munro hauled himself into the Defender, placed the dog on his lap, and buckled up as West pulled her phone from her hip.

'Voicemail,' she said. 'It's Duncan, sounds like he's in a hurry. He says McClure and Miller were in the pub and as soon as Miller discovered he was a cop, he legged it.'

'I'm not surprised,' said Munro, 'that fellow has a pathological hatred of authority.'

'Probably stems from his childhood,' said West, raising a hand. 'Duncan's going back to the pub, he reckons he's ID'd one of the blokes who gatecrashed Meena's gaff. He's going to bring him in.'

'Well, I hope he's careful,' said Munro. 'If he winds up in hospital, I'll not be able to visit him with a dog in tow.'

West clipped her phone to the windscreen, opened the sat nav, and keyed in the address of the garage just as Dougal's name appeared on the screen.

'Yes mate,' she said, 'what's up?'

'Where are you, miss?'

'We're on our way to Somerset Road.'

'Well, turn around!' said Dougal, excitedly. 'Gordon Miller, he's just been nabbed by traffic.'

'What? Blinding! How'd they manage that?'

'He was speeding and ANPR threw up a match to what we have of the index number for the hatchback, and you'll never guess, I was right after all! It's an Aygo!'

'Well, there's a surprise,' said West. 'Where is he now?'

'He's on the bypass just outside Kilmarnock.'

'Okay, tell uniform to hold him there. We're on our way.'

* * *

As an underage drinker knocking about the dive bars of his hometown, Duncan was used to downing several pints within an hour but was nonetheless surprised to find two empty glasses on the table with Fraser halfway through a third, well on his way to getting blootered.

'Oh, you're back!' said McClure as he sat beside her. 'He's still not here.'

'No, he's not answering his phone, either,' said Duncan, 'I thought I'd give him a wee bit longer. That's some thirst you've got on you, pal, have you been at the anchovies again?'

Fraser, stony-faced, glared at Duncan before breaking into a smile.

'Very good,' he said, raising his glass. 'Actually, I lay off the booze during the week so I've five days of catching up to do.'

'Looks like you've sorted day one, already.'

'Tommy,' said McClure, 'this is…'

'Duncan. Duncan will do.'

'He's waiting on Nav, a wee bit of business.'

'Oh, aye?' said Fraser, draining his glass. 'That'll be under-the-counter business, then.'

'No, no,' said Duncan. 'It's all above board. He's buying my motor.'

'He's winding you up. Unless he's turning it into a pedal car.'

'From what I've heard, I'm beginning to think I'm wasting my time.'

'I told you,' said McClure, 'you should pop over to his house.'

'Aye, maybe I will, but your pal left without giving me the address.'

'No danger, Tommy will tell you, he knows where he lives.'

'I do,' said Fraser. 'In fact, I'm of a mind to pop round there, myself.'

'Why's that?' said Duncan.

'He's into us for a couple of hundred.'

'Us?'

'Me and Gordon.'

'Stitched you up, has he?'

'He bought some gear,' said Fraser, 'and he's not coughed up. Actually, you look like the kind of fella who might be interested.'

'In what?'

Fraser glanced over his shoulder, pushed his empty glass to one side, and leaned across the table.

'Maryjane,' he said, softly. 'You know, weed. *Waccy-baccy.*'

'So, Nav's into that as well?'

'He's pretty much got the Uni sewn up. So, are you interested or not?'

Acutely aware that once-in-a-lifetime offers were few and far between, Duncan, trying his best not to smile, pondered for a moment before seizing the opportunity with both hands.

'Aye, go on, then,' he said, 'but not here.'

'Of course not here!' said Fraser. 'I'm not a dafty.'

'I've got the motor outside.'

Duncan turned to McClure and gave her a crafty wink.

'Recreational use,' he said, as he stood. 'No harm done, eh?'

'Oh, I've seen nothing,' said McClure. 'Nothing at all.'

* * *

Feeling the effects of three pints of lager on an empty stomach, Fraser, teetering on his feet, followed Duncan across the car park and hollered as he clocked the Audi.

'Oh, you beauty!' he said. 'That's pure class, that. See here, pal, that's not for the likes of Nav. No, no, that would do me. We should have a chat later; I might be able to take it off your hands.'

'Aye, okay,' said Duncan. 'Why not?'

Fraser slumped in the back seat and, after much puffing and sighing as he fumbled in his pockets, held out his palm to reveal a small, plastic bag containing 3.5 grams of weed.

'Here you go,' he said. 'Best of gear. Twenty quid.'

Duncan reached for his hand, slipped a cuff around his wrist, and quickly clipped the other to the handrail.

'Thomas Fraser,' he said, 'I am Detective Sergeant Reid and I'm arresting you under Section 1 of the Criminal Justice Act for supplying an illegal drug and I believe that keeping you in custody is necessary and proportionate for the purposes of bringing you before a court. Do you understand?'

Chapter 25

Had the task of clearing the contents of the office been assigned to West, the entire place would have been emptied with the brutal efficiency of a team of refuse collectors clearing a condemned house. However, with Dougal at the helm, the most valuable items were fastidiously swathed in several layers of bubble-wrap and sealed in a box marked 'Fragile – Handle With Care'.

She sat, arms folded, with her feet on the desk, and nodded towards the box.

'What's in that one?' she said. 'Is that all the laptops, and the phones, and stuff?'

'No, no,' said Dougal, 'that's the kettle and the ginger nuts, the chocolate digestives, the tea, the coffee, and the sugar. Oh, and a box of dog biscuits. I'll do the hardware just before we leave.'

'I'm not sure that's such a good idea,' said West. 'The way things are at the moment, we can't afford to be without. Can you set the macs up somewhere else?'

'Aye, no bother. But where?'

'What about Elliot's office? Has he gone?'

'I think so.'

'Good, we'll commandeer that, then. He won't even know we've been. Now, I wonder how much longer Duncan's going to be.'

'That,' said Munro, 'will all depend on Mr Fraser's inebriated state of mind. Alcohol has a habit of inducing one of two extremes: either unprecedented co-operation, or unwarranted aggression; so, let's hope it's the former.'

'Well, while we wait,' said West, 'you can bring us up to speed with what you've been up to. Any progress?'

'Aye, plenty, miss,' said Dougal. 'Although, it wasn't easy. Hunter's solicitor takes law-abiding to the extreme, especially when it comes to client confidentiality.'

'Well, that's his job,' said Munro, 'you cannae accuse the fellow of being obstinate for simply carrying out his duties.'

'Maybe not, but we are dealing with extenuating circumstances, boss. Anyhow, I wheedled it out of him in the end.'

'Wheedled what, exactly?'

'Okay,' said Dougal, 'remember the emails I found on his computer? Well, they had nothing to do with the purchase of their villa. Ross Hunter was changing his will.'

'Ooh, something juicy at last!' said West. 'Come on, then, who's got the winning ticket?'

'Well, it's not his wife, Eileen Hunter. His son, Kieran, gets a lump sum, but that's being held in a trust until he's twenty-one. Everything else goes to… Peggy McClure.'

West glanced at Munro, stood up, and walked around the table as she pondered McClure's prospective windfall.

'You know what?' she said, wagging her finger. 'I bet that crafty cow's known about this all along. Right, Dougal, two things; first, we need a warrant for her gaff, and we need it now.'

'Miss.'

'Then, sort out some back-up, and get your backside over there, as quick as you can.'

'Me?'

'Well, who else have we got? I'm about to interview Miller, and Duncan's still with Fraser.'

'Boss, I don't suppose…'

'Oh, no,' said Munro, with a smirk. 'I'm retired, laddie. I'm not laying myself open to a charge of impersonating a police officer, not for anyone.'

'Aye, but you wouldn't be,' said Dougal, 'I mean, you're a bona-fide volunteer, like a special.'

'But unlike a special, I have no powers of enforcement. Besides, I have a dog to look after.'

'What's all the commotion?' said Duncan as he swaggered through the door. 'I can hear you down the corridor.'

'Ah, my saviour!' said West. 'Duncan, before you give us the SP on Fraser, would you mind nipping over to McClure's gaff?'

'Aye, no bother. What's the story?'

'Ross Hunter has made her the sole beneficiary in his will, well, as good as, anyway, and I've got a hunch she knew about it. Also, she's pretty tight with Gordon Miller, too tight, if you ask me.'

'Okay, but what's Miller got to do with it?'

'It's looking like he's the one who clobbered Hunter.'

'Oh, this is coming together nicely,' said Duncan. 'So, do we have a warrant for McClure's house?'

'Dougal's sorting it now but we can't hang around, you'll have to blag it. Right, you need to get a move on so tell us quick, what's the deal with Fraser?'

'He's having a wee lie down,' said Duncan, 'but he's not going anywhere, except court, that is.'

'How d'you mean?'

'It seems Fraser and Gordon Miller had a wee side-line going, pushing weed. Navinder Singh-Gill was one of their favourite customers, and he sold it on to Tarif Khan who's been flogging it round the university campus.'

'So how did you nick him?'

'He tried flogging some to me, so I've done him for supply and possession.'

'Top man!' said West. 'So, we've got him until Monday, at least?'

'Aye, right enough, but that's not all. He's admitted being with Miller when they went to Meena's house but he's not saying any more than that, at least, not until he's sobered up.'

'Well, we've got our hands full, then,' said West, 'because Miller's downstairs, too. We're holding him on suspicion of manslaughter.'

'Has he been processed?'

'Yup, all sorted; prints, DNA samples, and incidentally, he's been temporarily relieved of a rather fancy watch.'

'Right, anything else, or is that it?'

'Just one thing,' said Duncan, 'we took four swabs when we booked Fraser, instead of two. One set's off to the lab, but I sent the other by courier to McLeod. He says he'll analyse it straight away so we've not long to wait to see if it matches the DNA on Meena's sheets.'

'And if it doesn't?'

'That leaves us with Miller. Either way, one of them's guilty, I'd stake my life on it.'

'That may be so,' said Munro, addressing the dog, 'but how will you prove it?'

'I'm not with you, chief. What more do we need?'

Munro, attributing a lack of experience for Duncan's failure to spot a glaring hole in the case for the prosecution, leaned across the table and spoke with the motivational encouragement of an enthusiastic tutor.

'See here, laddie,' he said, smiling softly, 'even if the DNA from the sheets matches that of Miller or Fraser, you have to ask yourself the question: does it prove that either of them is guilty of the charge of rape? And the answer is no. At best, it will prove that one of them is guilty of committing an act of depravity while Meena lay in her bed, and as it stands, the best you can hope for, is a verdict of not proven.'

'Don't you mean not guilty?' said West.

'No, no,' said Dougal. 'You see, miss, under Scottish law there are three possible verdicts for an offence of this nature: guilty, not guilty, and not proven. Not proven means the evidence isn't strong enough to secure a conviction, but it doesn't mean the alleged perpetrator is innocent.'

'So,' said Munro, 'the only way you can ensure that one of those chaps is on the receiving end of a custodial, is to get Meena Singh-Gill to make a sworn statement naming her attacker, or convince her to stand up in court. Now, is she certain of her assailant's identity?'

'Aye, she is,' said Duncan. 'According to Tarif Khan, she knows exactly who it is, but she's simply not saying.'

'Then you have to try again,' said Munro, 'and if she's worried about repercussions, then reassure her that she's nothing to fear. Tell her that Miller and Fraser will be behind bars for a good few years. And one more thing, you need to tell her now.'

'Roger that,' said Duncan, as he made for the door. 'I'll be back in a tick.'

* * *

Duncan, chastising himself for failing to spot the fundamental flaw in his assessment of the evidence, sat at the top of the stairwell feeling relieved that he hadn't got as far as filing a report with the fiscal.

'Ash,' he said. 'It's DS Reid, are you okay, pal?'

'Aye, not bad, Sergeant. I hear Meena paid you a visit.'

'She did, thanks for swinging that, but here's the thing, it's not enough.'

'How so?'

'Can you talk? I mean, are you somewhere private?'

'Aye, I'm with Tarif,' said Ash. 'We're at his place.'

'Good, then put me on speaker, he should hear this, too.'

'Okay, fire away.'

'Well, on the plus side,' said Duncan, 'you'll be pleased to know that the two numpties who crashed your party are now in custody.'

'Nice one, folk like that should be in a zoo.'

'Now, I know you've told me this before but I need to know for sure if Meena can identify her attacker.'

'You mean she's not told you herself?'

'She's not told me anything.'

'Well, she can,' said Ash. 'She's not told me either, but she did say she knew who it was.'

'Okay, see here, Ash, I need her to say as much because even if we get the result we want from forensics, it's not going to prove their guilt; they could walk away. And there's something else that could go against her.'

'What's that?'

'Tarif, you said Meena took herself off to bed because she was hammered, is that right?'

'Well, maybe not hammered,' said Tarif. 'I might have exaggerated a wee bit, but she'd had a few. How can that go against her?'

'Because her attacker could claim that what happened was consensual, and that she can't remember because she was drunk.'

'Oh, no, that's not right,' said Ash. 'See here, Sergeant, she may have had a drink or two, but she's not the kind of girl who'd jump into bed with anyone, let alone one of those Neanderthals.'

'I get that,' said Duncan, 'which is why she has to name him, either in a sworn statement or by standing up in court.'

'Fat chance of that happening. There's no way she'd want her name bandied about the town, and then there's her mother, if she ever got wind of what happened…'

'Okay, just hold it there,' said Duncan. 'Just give me a moment.'

Whilst aware that Meena's reluctance to name her attacker was not unusual for victims of a sexual assault, Duncan remained frustrated, nonetheless, by the possibility that her attacker could walk free, and played the only other card he had left in his hand.

'Listen,' he said. 'Tarif, Ash. Do you think she'd testify if she knew she had her family on her side?'

'She has,' said Ash. 'She knows we're right behind her.'

'Aye, but what I mean is, would she feel more comfortable if she knew you were testifying as well?'

'How would that work?'

Duncan, without wanting to sound as if he was delivering an ultimatum, took a deep breath and dived in.

'You fellas enjoy a wee smoke,' he said. 'Am I right?'

'Well…'

'Listen, Tarif, I know for a fact you've been flogging gear all over the campus, so now's not the time to play the innocent, do you get what I'm saying?'

'Aye, okay,' said Tarif, 'so we enjoy a smoke, what of it?'

'Who did you get it from? Was it Nav?'

Duncan threw his head back and closed his eyes as he waited for the painful pause to end.

'Aye,' said Tarif. 'It was Nav.'

'Okay, so here's the thing. I know who Nav's supplier was, the question is, do you?'

'It was them,' said Ash, 'it was the two fellas who showed up at the house.'

'And would you be willing to put that in a statement?'

'Oh, I'm not sure about that; that would mean…'

'Oh, lighten up, pal!' said Duncan, impatiently. 'Listen, they're going down for dealing anyway. If you put your weight behind us, they'll go down for even longer but more importantly, if Meena knows you're doing that, it may just be enough to convince her to do the same. So, what do you say?'

'I'll do it,' said Tarif, excitedly, 'after what Nav put me through, I'd even plug in the chair if you had one.'

'Ash?'

'Well, if Tarif's up for it, then, aye, okay. I will, too.'

'Lads,' said Duncan, allowing himself the widest of grins, 'you have just made one detective very happy. Okay, so, will I have a word with Meena, or would you rather have a go yourselves?'

'I think maybe it's better coming from us,' said Ash. 'When should we do it?'

'The sooner the better,' said Duncan. 'And listen, you're to call me as soon as she's made a decision, either way, okay?'

Chapter 26

As a young boy tethered to the apron strings of an over-protective mother, Gordon Miller – psychologically scarred by the torrent of abuse he'd suffered at the hands of his cruel classmates whose daily taunts questioned his intelligence as well as his physicality – had grown up in the belief that attack was the best form of defence; a view which manifested itself not as a sharp retort based on observational wit, but as a swift right hand to the cheek.

However, when faced with a single opponent in contests of a cerebral nature he would, through a fear of inadequacy, overestimate his intellectual acuity and, as a consequence, arrogantly dismiss the offer of legal representation.

'Is this not a bit extreme for a poxy wee speeding ticket?' he said, scowling at West.

'I'd say speeding was the least of your worries, right now.'

'Oh, aye?' said Miller, rubbing his wrists. 'Well, you've a few of your own – police brutality being one of them.'

'A big bloke like you whining about a teensy-weensy bruise from a pair of handcuffs?' said West. 'You should file a complaint. So, you were in a bit of hurry, weren't you, Mr Dickie?'

'It's Miller.'

'Sorry?'

'I go by the name of Miller.'

'Not according to national records, you don't. Or the tax office. Or the electoral register. Frankly, I don't see what your problem is. It's a common enough name.'

'You've not had to live with it.'

'Well, you're a grown man now,' said West. 'I think it's about time you got over it, don't you? Now, while we're on the subject of genealogy, what does the name "Hunter" mean to you?'

'Nothing.'

'Are you sure? Hunter? Mr Ross Hunter?'

'I've told you before,' said Miller. 'I've never heard of him.'

'Well, that's odd,' said West. 'Because that's not what Peggy says.'

'Peggy?'

'Yup. She can talk the hind legs off a donkey when she wants to.'

'What's she been saying?'

'Never you mind,' said West. 'You're pretty close, aren't you? You and Peggy?'

Miller narrowed his eyes and glared at West.

'We're friends,' he said. 'Workmates.'

'Of course you are. You've got a bit of a temper, haven't you? Some might say you're a bit of a loose cannon. So, tell me, what made you do it? Was it jealousy?'

'I'm not with you.'

'Oh, come on,' said West, intent on pushing him to the edge, 'you're not stupid. Peggy was having it away with Ross Hunter. Is that why you went after him? To scare him off because he was muscling in on the bird you fancied? That must have been a right wind-up, having to look her in the eye every day, all the time knowing she was jumping into bed with someone else.'

Miller sat bolt upright and threw his arms in the air.

'Aye, okay!' he said, raising his voice. 'I was jealous, so I gave him a wee tap! I told him to back off! There, are you happy now?'

Sensing Miller was on the ropes but had yet to hit the canvas, West, smirking in an effort to rile him further, leaned back and crossed her arms.

'I'm never happy,' she said. 'And do you know why? Because nothing's ever quite as it seems. Because never, in my entire career, have I had someone confess to a crime less than five minutes into an interview. So, you gave him a tap. Weren't you worried about getting caught?'

'I hadn't thought about it.'

'Well, that's obvious,' said West. 'The way you wandered in and out of his shop, anyone would think you'd popped in for a newspaper. What about Peggy? Did she know you'd paid him a visit?'

Miller, looking as though he'd been asked to state the chemical formula for barium hydroxide, frowned as he pondered the question.

'No,' he said, lowering his voice. 'She has no idea.'

'Really?'

'Aye. You keep her out of this. Listen, I've told you what you needed to know, so what's the problem? If you're going to do me for GBH, or assault, or whatever you call it, then just get on with it. I'll probably get a suspended anyway.'

'Oh, that's highly unlikely,' said West.

'You think so?'

'Yup.'

'Why?'

'Because I'm not going to do you for GBH. I'm going to do you for manslaughter.'

West, intrigued by the transformation, cocked her head to one side and regarded Miller sympathetically as his expression changed from that of a howling hothead to one of a vulnerable, young boy left to fend for himself.

'I'm not with you,' he said, nervously. 'Manslaughter?'

'Afraid so,' said West. 'Ross Hunter's dead. He died from his injuries. To be precise, he had a bleed on the brain.'

'Oh, no,' said Miller. 'No, no, that's not right, that wasn't meant to happen! I only gave the fella a wee tap!'

'Well, it did the job. And what's more, you've left a kid without a father, and a wife without a husband. I bet you feel crap, now.'

'You listen to me,' said Miller, his eyes darting about the room as he scratched the back of his head, 'I'm not a murderer, okay? I did not intend to kill anyone! Have you got that? See here, I'm not doing this on my own! If I'm going down for manslaughter, then she's coming with me!'

'Who's coming with you?'

'Peggy, of course!

'Peggy?'

'Aye! Are you not listening? It was all her idea!'

'Oh, nice try,' said West, 'but that's not going to get you off the hook, the fact of the matter is…'

'Facts! I'll give you a wee fact! Ross Hunter fancied the wee pants off Peggy and she knew it!'

'So, what are you saying? That she led him on?'

'Aye! Like a horse to water! It was all a game to her!'

'Why?' said West. 'What was she after?'

'What do you think? His money!'

'There's a novelty.'

Miller, his hands trembling, took a deep breath as he tried to calm his nerves.

'Okay,' he said. 'Ross Hunter told Peggy that as soon as he got a divorce, they could marry. He was that loved up, he said he was going to put a deposit on a wee house for the pair of them in Mallorca. He even said he'd changed his will so if anything happened, she'd get the lot.'

Despite the fact that she could hear a referee in the back of her head declaring the fight a knock-out, West, needing a few more details to be sure of a conviction, maintained a look of utter boredom and stared vacuously into space.

'Sorry,' she said, stifling a fake yawn, 'but that's all sounding a bit far-fetched to me. If he was offering her all that, why did she get you involved?'

'Because,' said Miller, 'she didn't want *all that*. She just wanted his money. Look, me and Peggy, we've been together a couple of years. She said if I took care of him, we'd be set for life.'

'Why didn't she do it herself?' said West. 'She's a clever lady, strong too. Surely she could've managed a bit of rat poison in his tea.'

'She said she was too close,' said Miller. 'If anyone started asking questions, then she'd be the first in the firing line, but there's no way they'd come after me.'

'Well, she got that wrong. So, what happened? With Hunter?'

Miller stared at West and shrugged his shoulders.

'I lost my bottle,' he said. 'When I went to his shop, he had his back to the door. I lifted the hammer and fair cacked myself, I couldn't do it. But then he turned around, and he went for me. The fella was only trying to defend himself; I'll not fault him for that, but I hit him. Accidentally. It wasn't intentional, it was just a wee tap, but he went down. I threw the hammer on the floor and I walked out.'

'So that's why you weren't bothered about being caught? Because you didn't think anything serious had happened?'

'I thought at best he'd have a wee headache. That's all.'

'Well, it's too late for aspirin,' said West, 'that's for sure, but you know what? Surprisingly enough, I believe you. And even more surprisingly, I actually feel a bit sorry for you. She's played you like a fiddle, hasn't she? You must feel like a right mug, but unfortunately, the law's the law. You'll be in court on Monday and oh, if it's any consolation, don't worry about Peggy, she'll be there, too.'

Miller sat cradling his face in his hands and gazed forlornly at West.

'I've messed up, haven't I?' he said despondently. 'So, is that me away then?'

West mustered a mediocre smile and nodded.

'How long?'

'Hard to say,' said West. 'It all depends on how good your brief is. If he can convince everyone that you acted under duress, that you were somehow coerced into it, then you might get a reduced sentence.'

'I see,' said Miller. 'No chance of a beer, is there? No, I thought not. So, what happens now? Do I just go back to my cell and wait?'

'Not yet. We've got one more matter to deal with.'

West stood up, slid her hands into her pockets, and leaned against the wall.

'Have you got any hobbies?' she said.

'Hobbies?'

'Yeah, you know, like football? Or fishing? Or gardening? I hear you're quite green-fingered.'

'Sorry?'

'Pot-plants. You like your pot-plants, don't you?'

'Oh, that,' said Miller, closing his eyes as the penny dropped. 'How did you know?'

'Your mate Tommy Fraser's just been done for dealing.'

'I see.'

'Apparently,' said West, 'you had a bit of a cash-flow problem. Is that why you went to see Nav at his house?'

'Christ, nothing gets past you, does it?'

'So?'

'Nav owed us some money,' said Miller.

'What for? Weed?'

'Aye.'

'So, what happened when you got to his house?'

'Nothing. As far as I can remember.'

'Actually, that's not quite true, is it?' said West. 'Quite a lot happened, so out with it. Time's marching on and I want my dinner.'

Miller paused for a moment, took a deep breath, and sighed.

'We got to his house,' he said. 'There was music playing, it sounded like he was having a party.'

'Was he expecting you?'

'No.'

'So, who was there? Apart from Nav.'

'His sister, his brother, and his brother's pal. A fella called Tarif.'

'And did you know them?' said West. 'I mean, had you met before?'

'Aye, but just to say hello to,' said Miller. 'No more than that.'

'You weren't very polite, were you? It's not the done thing to be abusive to people when you're a guest in their home.'

'That wasn't me. That was Tommy.'

'Has he got something against gays, then?'

'I don't think he meant it. It was probably just the booze talking.'

'The funny thing about booze,' said West, 'is it has a habit of telling the truth. So, you were drunk, were you? You and Fraser?'

'We'd had a few, aye.'

'So, what happened next?'

'His brother and his pal got offended, they took themselves off.'

'I don't blame them,' said West. 'And what about his sister, Meena? Did she get the hump, too?'

'Aye. She went to bed.'

'Then what?'

'I opened a beer and asked Nav for the cash.'

'And what did he say?'

'He said he was skint. Then he sat down and put the telly on.'

'And your mate Fraser,' said West. 'Where was he while all this was going on?'

'I've no idea. He said he was nipping upstairs to use the lavvy, then I fell asleep.'

'And what time did he wake you up?'

'About fifteen minutes later. He was in a hurry, he said we had to leave.'

West took a few paces forward and perched herself on the edge of the desk.

'Have you any idea what happened while Fraser was upstairs? Have you any idea what he was up to?'

Miller bit his lip and looked away.

'Listen, there's no point trying to cover for him, he's already got one foot on the gallows.'

'I sort of guessed,' said Miller sheepishly. 'When we left, Tommy said something about going into the girl's room, but I told him to shut up. I said I didn't want to know.'

'You're sure about that, are you?' said West. 'I mean, you'd had a few jars, maybe you're getting confused. Are you sure you weren't with him? Are you sure you didn't join in?'

'Away!' said Miller. 'That's sick! Listen, I've a few bad habits, I'll give you that, but I'm not a…'

'And Fraser is?'

'You've seen him yourself! He's not exactly catch-of-the-day! He gets it any way he can!'

'I've got news for you, sunshine,' said West as she terminated the interview, 'you're not exactly Brad Pitt, yourself.'

Chapter 27

With the prospect of relocating to some Godforsaken corner of the Outer Hebrides for the sake of a paltry pay packet consigned to history, Duncan – preoccupied with sealing the fate of an unidentified rapist to justify his worth – deferred his girlfriend's enticing offer of a celebratory takeaway and a bottle of plonk, and contemplated instead the wisdom of buying a black car as he sat wilting beneath a searing sun watching the house for any signs of movement.

Assuming the building to be empty, he made his way up the path, rang the bell, and reached for his lock-picks just as McClure, who'd swapped her work clothes for a pair of skin-tight ski pants and a Lycra vest, opened the door looking, wrinkles aside, like Barbie on steroids.

'Sergeant Reid,' she said with a pout. 'The way you've been following me around, anyone would think you're after a date.'

'Oh, I've no time for that,' said Duncan, 'anyhow, I thought you'd be in the pub with your pals.'

'Pals? Fine friends they turned out to be. They both walked out the door and disappeared into thin air, leaving me on my tod.'

'Probably another dodgy deal,' said Duncan. 'Am I interrupting something? Only you're all dolled up.'

'No, no, I'm just getting myself together,' said McClure. 'What can I do for you, anyway? Are you after Nav?'

'No, I've given up on him. The fact is, I'm here to take a wee look around your house.'

'Oh?'

'Don't ask me,' said Duncan, 'I'm not even meant to be working. It's a part of the investigation, I'm just following orders.'

'And what is it you're looking for, exactly?'

Duncan shot her a disarming smile and shrugged his shoulders.

'It's that boss of yours, isn't it?' said McClure. 'She's got it in for me, I'm telling you. Well, come away through, help yourself, I've nothing to hide but you'll have to excuse me, I've some packing to do.'

'Packing?'

'Aye. What with Gordy and Tommy standing me up, I thought I'd make the most of the weekend and visit my sister.'

'Oh, very nice,' said Duncan as he glanced around the lounge. 'And where does she stay? Anywhere nice?'

'Aye, Troon.'

'There's a coincidence.'

'Wee Bobby likes it,' said McClure as she grabbed a pile of laundry from the kitchen. 'He can run about in the woods, or on the beach if it's not too hot. I'm away upstairs if you want to follow.'

'I'm right behind you,' said Duncan, reaching for his phone. 'Bear with me a minute.'

The text from West was brief and to the point: 'bring her in, sus of A&A'.

Not wanting to cause a scene, Duncan made his way upstairs to find Bobby the Bruce lying beside an open suitcase on top of the bed.

'He knows we're off,' said McClure, folding a pile of tee shirts. 'If he could jump in there, he would.'

'Folk underestimate the intelligence of dogs,' said Duncan. 'They could actually teach us a thing or two. Do you mind?'

McClure looked up as Duncan pointed at the wardrobe.

'Aye, no bother,' she said, 'just don't give me any tips on makeovers, you'll not find anything fashionable in there.'

Turning his back on McClure, Duncan opened the door and leafed through the assorted coats and sweaters hanging from the rail, making a mental note of the men's shirts and folded pairs of jeans crammed to one side before closing it again.

'Toiletries,' said McClure as she shot to the bathroom, 'and I'm just about there.'

Ignoring the bottle of Calvin Klein aftershave and the disposable razor, she grabbed a handful of cosmetics, a toothbrush, and a small make-up mirror, tossed them into a wash bag, and returned to the bedroom.

'Right, that's me,' she said as she zipped the case. 'My handbag's downstairs so I'll get that on the way out. Are you done? Did you find what you were looking for?'

'Aye, I think so,' said Duncan. 'Are you wanting a lift anywhere?'

'Oh, no. That's too much to ask.'

'Away, it's no bother. Here, I'll take the case, you grab Bobby.'

'That's smashing. Thanks very much.'

Smarting at the blast of heat as he opened the door, Duncan, concerned for the welfare of the dog, switched the air-con to full, listened for the reassuring clunk of the central locking, and slowly pulled away.

'Oh, listen,' he said, 'I almost forgot. I have to make a wee stop on the way, are you okay with that?'

'Aye, I guess so,' said McClure. 'Will it take long?'

'No, no. I have to stop by the office, that's all.'

Alarmed by the inexplicable rise of butterflies in her belly, McClure fumbled nervously with her watch and glanced furtively at the back of Duncan's head.

'Maybe it's best if you drop me at the bus station, after all,' she said, forcing a smile. 'I'm in a wee bit of a hurry.'

'Oh, it's too late now,' said Duncan, 'that's impossible.'

'Don't be daft. Look, anywhere will do. You could drop me here.'

'Sorry.'

'Why not?'

'Because Miss McClure, I'm arresting you under section 1 of the Criminal Justice Act on suspicion of aiding and abetting in the murder of Ross Hunter. You're not obliged to say anything but anything you do say will be noted and may be used in evidence. Do you understand?'

Chapter 28

Crammed into DCI's Elliot's tiny office, Dougal and West sat shoulder to shoulder with one completing a report for the Procurator Fiscal detailing Tommy Fraser's horticultural habits, as the other searched online for any last minute bargains in the summer sales while Munro, looking like a candidate for the last rites, sat catching flies in the easy chair with an equally dozy Murdo curled up on his lap.

West looked up and smiled as Duncan, exhausted from running around town in pursuit of Meena Singh-Gill's attackers and the apprehension of a devious Peggy McClure, trudged into the office with a Border Terrier under his arm.

'I'm in desperate need of a beer,' he said as he placed Bobby the Bruce on the desk. 'McClure's booked in, miss. Are you going to see to her now?'

'You're having a laugh,' said West. 'Have you seen the time? As Lewis Carroll wrote, "*the time has come, the walrus said, to talk of many things*", like the benefits of a decent claret and a 16-ounce steak.'

'Hear, hear,' said Munro, roused by the mention of supper. 'What's that wee fellow doing here?'

'I'm not sure what to do with him, chief. He can't stay with McClure, that's for sure.'

'Right enough, and as he'll not be seeing his mother for the foreseeable, the poor chap's bound to be traumatised.'

'That's what I thought,' said Duncan. 'Dougal, will you not take him?'

'Me? No, no. He's liable to take a chunk out of my arm while I'm asleep.'

'Away! He's as soft as anything. You could hang a pork chop about your neck and cover yourself in Bisto and he'd still not bite.'

'The answer's no.'

'I think you're forgetting who actually owns the dog,' said Munro. 'You'd best talk to McClure first, she may have friends or family he could stay with.'

'And if not?'

'Then I can think of no-one better qualified to look after the hound than yourself.'

'Oh, it's too much for me to take on,' said Duncan, 'with the hours I keep, it wouldn't be fair.'

'Well, why not have a word with McClure first?' said West. 'If push comes to shove then maybe you could take him for now; after all, it is the weekend.'

'Chief, do you not think Murdo would enjoy the company?'

'One's plenty,' said Munro. 'Thanking you.'

'So, come on then,' said West, 'what's the deal with McClure?'

'Well, she's not living alone,' said Duncan. 'Her wardrobe's full of men's gear, and there's stuff in the bathroom, too.'

'And I can almost guarantee it all belongs to Miller,' said West, 'and guess what? Not only has he pleaded guilty to the attack on Ross Hunter, he says McClure put him up to it.'

'So, if he got caught, she'd walk away? A manipulator as well as a thief. Okay, I'm going to have word with the

208

Black Widow about the wee man, then I'm going to call it a day.'

'Hold on,' said West, 'before you go, I want you to come next door with me. You've got some visitors.'

'Visitors?'

'Yup, but first, brace yourself for some news. We got a call from McLeod. He found a match for the DNA off Meena's bed sheets.'

'Get in there, you beauty!' said Duncan, punching the air. 'So, Fraser's…'

'It's not Fraser.'

Duncan, reeling from the revelation, stared wide-eyed at West with a look of utter disbelief smeared across his face.

'It's Miller,' she said. 'If there's one thing that can be said about the bloke, he certainly knows how to keep himself busy. Come on.'

* * *

Milling about the vast, empty office like a bunch of lost souls who'd got the wrong address for an all-night rave, Meena Singh-Gill, her brother Ash, and Tarif Khan, all smiled in unison as Duncan, with West in his wake, waltzed through the door.

'Well, if it's not The Three Musketeers,' he said. 'What's all this about?'

'We thought we'd like to tell you in person,' said Meena. 'It's the least we could do.'

'I'm not with you,' said Duncan. 'Tell me what?'

'We'll do it. I'll do it. I'll tell you who attacked me.'

'Well, this is a turn up for the books!' said Duncan. 'Not that I'm complaining, mind, but why the sudden change of heart?'

'Nav.'

'Nav? But he's banged up, or he soon will be.'

'Exactly,' said Meena. 'Which means he can't touch me. Which means I no longer have anything to worry about.'

'Hold on, hen, you're losing me. You'll have to explain.'

Ash, keen to cement his role as defender of the family name, took his hands from his pockets and stepped forward.

'You see, Sergeant, Meena refused to say anything before, not because of shame, or embarrassment, but because she was scared. Because Nav had threatened her.'

'Are you serious?'

'Nav knew exactly what happened that night,' said Ash, 'but he told Meena to keep her mouth shut or she'd land him in a spot of bother.'

'With Miller and Fraser?'

'Aye.'

'So, they can get a bit heavy?'

'That's one way of putting it,' said Ash. 'They told Nav they'd do him over if word ever got out about the rape, or the fact that they were dealing, and when they say "do over", it often means losing the use of your legs.'

'But?'

'But when Meena came to us, Tarif went ballistic. He and Nav had a massive blow-out which ended with Tarif saying he was going to report him to the police.'

'Is that right?' said Duncan.

'Aye,' said Tarif, 'every word. I know I'm not family, but see here, Sergeant, I've spent my entire life hiding away or being bullied for being gay, and I wasn't about to let those two homophobic neds get the better of Meena, no way.'

'And the only reason we couldn't tell you everything before,' said Ash, 'is because we didn't want Nav going after Meena. It was her choice, and we had to respect that.'

West, refraining from interrupting, watched as Duncan, hand raised, slowly paced the floor.

'Okay,' he said, 'so let me get this straight. What you're actually saying is that Nav knew nothing about your vow of silence? He had no idea you'd decided to keep things to yourselves?'

'None,' said Tarif. 'The man was raging. He thought I was going to go to the police and shop all three of them.'

'And he couldn't take the risk, could he? He had to be sure you'd keep quiet, so that's why he attacked you?'

'Aye.'

'Well, you've done the right thing,' said West, 'you should be proud of yourselves. At the very least, you've probably stopped someone else falling victim to those louts. All I can say is, thanks.'

'No bother,' said Ash. 'I just hope they get what they deserve.'

'Oh, they will. So, are you up for making a statement?'

'Whenever you like,' said Meena. 'We're ready when you are.'

'Well, it's getting a bit late, now,' said West, 'and to be honest, after the day we've had, we're all feeling a bit frazzled. How about first thing tomorrow? I can send a car to pick you up.'

'Perfect,' said Meena, 'so, would you like to know who it was?'

'I'm ahead of you there, hen,' said Duncan, with a grin, 'we already know, and I can promise you this, he'll not being seeing daylight for years to come.'

Epilogue

Whilst the southern half of the country was already cloaked in darkness, Munro and West, keen to make the most of a pleasantly balmy evening, left the cars at the office in favour of a casual thirty minute stroll along the river back to West's apartment on North Harbour Street where, in a little over two hours, they could witness the spectacle of another captivating Caledonian sunset.

'We could break out the best china,' said West, 'and have tea on the terrace.'

'By which you mean, supper on the balcony.'

'Same thing. *La cena al fresco.*'

'I'm after a steak, Charlie. Not spaghetti and meatballs. Speaking of meatballs, how's Duncan shaping up?'

'You've seen for yourself, he's playing a blinder.'

'Aye, I'll not argue with that,' said Munro. 'Fear, it has a habit of bringing out the best in folk.'

'The funny thing is, I thought there'd be some tension between him and Dougal, you know, now that he's a DS too; but you were right, they suit each other down to the ground.'

'You cannae have brains without the brawn, lassie. Not in this game.'

'True, but he's got a bit of both,' said West. 'Give it a year and it wouldn't surprise me if he knocked me out of a job.'

Munro came to an abrupt halt as the tenacious terrier stopped to inspect the scent of the hedgerow.

'And the affair with this Miller chap,' he said, rubbing his shoulder, 'has that been put to bed?'

'Yup. The weasel even tried to stitch-up his mate over the rape, he swore blind that he was out cold on the sofa while Fraser was upstairs doing the deed.'

'But?'

'But a quick word with Nav soon put paid to that. He said it was Fraser who was snoozing on the sofa and McLeod confirmed it all with a DNA match to Miller using the samples from Meena's bed sheets.'

'And Meena Singh-Gill,' said Munro, 'she's finally agreed to give a statement?'

'Not just her,' said West, 'her brother and Tarif Khan are joining in too, which means Miller, Fraser and Nav probably won't get less than sixty years between them.'

'And Miss McClure? I'm guessing you threw the book at her?'

'I did,' said West, 'unfortunately it wasn't a hardback. She'll definitely go down for coercion but I'm going to see if the fiscal will buy a charge of wasting police time, too. She's done nothing but mislead this investigation from the word go.'

'You're not keen on the woman, are you, Charlie?'

'Nah, not really. She's a liar and a cheat, but that doesn't bother me anymore, and do you know why?'

West turned to Munro and grinned.

'Ross Hunter never got around to signing his will,' she said. 'She doesn't get a blooming penny! It all goes to his son and his wife!'

'Well, I suppose there is some justice in this world, after all,' said Munro, 'but the person I feel sorry for, is the wee dog. I've given it some thought and maybe having two wouldnae be so bad. As Duncan said, it would be company for wee Murdo, here.'

'No need to worry on that score, Jimbo. It turns out McClure does have a sister after all. She lives in a place called Portobello, wherever that is.'

'Edinburgh,' said Munro. 'Well, that's a relief. At least he'll be by the sea, he'll enjoy that. As will Murdo.'

'What do you mean?'

'Home,' said Munro. 'I cannae stay with you indefinitely.'

'Of course you can.'

'No, no. It's about time I introduced this chap to the creature comforts of his master's home. I'm away tomorrow. And you?'

'Well,' said West, mildly saddened by his impending departure, 'I've got to get statements from Meena and the others, then I have to go through the motions with McClure.'

'Even so, you should be clear by noon.'

'Yeah, I would have thought so.'

'Good, that's settled then,' said Munro. 'You're to bring yourself down to Carsethorn and I shall treat you and wee Murdo to supper in the pub.'

'Alright,' said West. 'You're on.'

'And in the morning, you can help me weed the garden.'

'I knew there'd be a catch.'

'There's no such thing as a free lunch, Charlie. Mark my words, there's no such thing as a free lunch.'

Character List

JAMES MUNRO (RETIRED) – Recovering from open-heart surgery, Munro, unable to relax without the stimuli of a convoluted case to occupy his mind, proves his worth when a complex investigation almost grinds to a halt.

DI CHARLOTTE WEST – Employing the methods of her mentor, West finally discovers how rational thought and a reliance on her instinct can prove invaluable when it comes to uncovering a web of deceit.

DS DOUGAL McCRAE – As an introverted night owl with a mind that operates like an algorithm, Dougal McCrae, peerless when it comes to combining technological know-how and hard facts, uncovers the shady side of a respectable business.

DS DUNCAN REID – The newly promoted DS with a maverick approach to policing goes all out to prove his worth when the threat of transferring to a new patch looms over his head.

DCI GEORGE ELLIOT – The ebullient DCI Elliot, with the help of Munro, takes on his superiors in an effort to secure the future of the department.

DR ANDY MCLEOD – Forensic pathologist Andy McLeod imparts some disturbing revelations when the amputated digits of a young male are discovered amongst the detritus at the local waste centre.

PEGGY McCLURE – A slender, bottle-blonde gym bunny with a taste for money and men, who knows what she wants, and usually gets it.

GORDON MILLER – An emotionally insecure grafter who's not afraid of hard work, or anyone who comes between him and his woman.

TOMMY FRASER – A pot-bellied fantasist with an eye for a deal and an unquenchable thirst who finds himself in the firing line when a colleague attempts to frame him for a heinous crime.

ROSS HUNTER – A doting father and a successful businessman wrapped up in a loveless marriage who finally finds solace in the arms of a teacher, although his plans for the future are short-lived.

EILEEN HUNTER – A wife and a mother who all but disowns her family for the finer things in life, abandons her home for a future fuelled by sun, sea, and sangria.

TARIF KHAN – An industrious student with a compassionate nature who becomes innocently embroiled in a cover-up by local dealers.

ASHAR SINGH-GILL – A workshy, armchair activist who, armed with a smartphone and several social media accounts, is willing to defend the rights of anyone except his brother.

NAVINDER SINGH-GILL – A small-time wheeler-dealer who fears for his life when his cohorts in crime take advantage of his naivety.

MEENA SINGH-GILL – A demure college girl with aspirations of becoming a frontline journalist has her world turned upside down when falling victim to her brother's errant ways.

If you enjoyed this book, please let others know by leaving a quick review on Amazon. Also, if you spot anything untoward in the paperback, get in touch. We strive for the best quality and appreciate reader feedback.

editor@thebookfolks.com

www.thebookfolks.com

ALSO BY PETE BRASSETT

SHE

With a serial killer on their hands, Scottish detective Munro and rookie sergeant West must act fast to trace a woman observed at the crime scene. Yet discovering her true identity, let alone finding her, proves difficult. Soon they realise the crime is far graver than either of them could have imagined.

AVARICE

A sleepy Scottish town, a murder in a glen. The local police chief doesn't want a fuss and calls in DI Munro to lead the investigation. But Munro is a stickler for procedure, and his sidekick Charlie West has a nose for a cover up. Someone in the town is guilty, will they find out who?

ENMITY

When it comes to frustrating a criminal investigation, this killer has all the moves. A spate of murders is causing havoc in a remote Scottish town. Enter Detective Inspector Munro to catch the red herrings and uncover an elaborate and wicked ruse.

DUPLICITY

When a foreign worker casually admits to the murder of a local businessman, detectives in a small Scottish town guess that the victim's violent death points to a more complex cause. Money appears to be a motive, but will anyone believe that they might be in fact dealing with a crime of passion?

TERMINUS

Avid fans of Scottish detective James Munro will be worrying it is the end of the line for their favourite sleuth when, battered and bruised following a hit and run, the veteran crime-solver can't pin down a likely suspect.

TALION

A boy finds a man's body on a beach. Police quickly suspect foul play when they discover he was part of a local drugs ring. With no shortage of suspects, they have a job pinning anyone down. But when links to a local business are discovered, it seems the detectives may have stumbled upon a much bigger crime than they could have imagined.

PERDITION

A man is found dead in his car. A goat is killed with a crossbow. What connects these events in a rural Scottish backwater? DI Charlotte West investigates in this gripping murder mystery that ends with a sucker punch of a twist.

RANCOUR

When the body of a girl found on a mountainside tests positive for a date rape drug, police suspect a local Lothario is responsible. He certainly had the means, motive and opportunity. But is this really such a cut and dry case? What are the detectives missing?

PENITENT

The shady past of a small town surfaces when a young woman is found murdered in a pool. As detectives investigate, a legacy of regret and resentment emerges. DI Munro and DI West must get to the bottom of the matter.

HUBRIS

When a dead sailor is found in a boat, detective Charlie West is tasked with finding out why. But getting answers from a tight-knit Scottish fishing community won't be easy, and besides, has the killer completely covered their tracks?

PENURY

James Munro is busy minding other people's business out of town when he stumbles upon an unfortunate DI Greg Byrne who is out of his depth dealing with a garish murder. Offering a helping hand, Munro soon realizes there are connections with a case closer to home. Will it be his new star pupil or his old protégé DI Charlie West who'll bring home the bacon?